MAGIC
TRANSFORMED

TWISTED CURSE BOOK FOUR

D. J. DALTON

deborah@djdalton.com

ISBN-13: 978-1-7368219-8-5

V isit **https://www.djdalton.com**, or use the QR code below, and subscribe to my newsletter to receive updates on new releases as well as other freebies. As a subscriber, you'll receive access to the free download of the novella prequel to the *Twisted Curse Series, The Dragon War*.

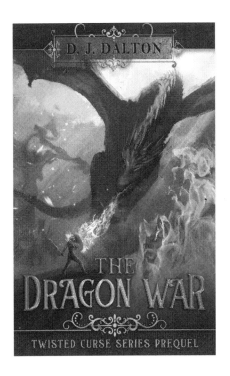

CONTENTS

CHAPTER ONE

KEREN

As Keren sprinted down the sidewalk next to the Circus Circus resort in Las Vegas, an acrid smell stung her nose and throat. Although dragons and sorcerers had agreed to a truce, fires continued to smolder all around the city from their vicious magic battles. Keren's legs burned, but she willed them to move faster.

"Stop!" she yelled.

A woman fox shifter, who had stormed past an inquisitor roadblock, dashed ahead of Keren at an unbelievable speed. The shifter wore a knee-length flower-print dress. A mixture of mud and blood covered her bare feet, showing she'd long abandoned her shoes.

When the shifter twisted to glance behind her, Keren saw her grimy, sweat-streaked face. Black-as-coal eyes betrayed the shifter's affliction of magic frenzy.

Witnessing the crazed and terrifying behavior of fox shifters infected with the disorder sent pangs of guilt through Keren. If she had known this would happen ... But the fox shifter cut off her thoughts when her upper lip curled into a snarl and she flung a hand toward Keren, producing a poorly aimed water-jet blast. The blast struck the resort's wall, causing bits of concrete to rain down on Keren from the impact.

Keren wrapped her arms around her head to protect herself. As she kept running, sharp-edged fragments dug into her skin. She weaved to avoid a sizable chunk that exploded when it hit the sidewalk.

The fox shifter ran around the corner of the resort. Wary of an ambush, Keren reached the corner and flattened herself against the wall. She peeked around the corner as another water jet sailed toward her. She pulled back, and the water-jet blast whooshed by and crashed into a restaurant across the street. It was a good thing the inquisitors had evacuated the public from the city. While crouching down, Keren peeked around the corner again. She saw the fox shifter racing away.

Keren bolted from her cover and continued the chase. She skidded to a halt when another fox shifter leapt out of a window and landed less than ten feet in front of her, blocking her path.

A low growl came from the male fox shifter's throat with each raspy exhale. His dark-blue security guard uniform hung in shredded strips from his body. A missing pant leg exposed multiple bleeding gashes. His ink-black eyes sent a chill down Keren's spine.

"I don't want to hurt you," she said as she raised her arm with her palm facing the shifter.

His muscles tensed, then he sprang forward.

"*Protegioum!*" Keren shouted.

A clear shield appeared seconds before the shifter's strike. She felt the force of his body push against her spell.

He bared his teeth, curled his hands into fists, and pounded on her shield. Each strike sent vibrations through her body. With this vicious barrage, she wouldn't be able to hold the spell for long.

"Stop!" Keren shouted. "I want to help you."

The words only made the shifter more frantic to reach her.

Her hand and arm quivered as she strained to hold the shield. Tiny black specks dotted the back of her extended hand and fingers. Although she came from a line of powerful sorcerers, she hadn't been trained in spell casting, which limited her stamina and her options.

From the right side, the woman fox shifter that Keren had been chasing barreled toward her. She must have circled back. Now Keren had to deal with two attackers.

The woman slid to a stop six feet from Keren's shield and raised both of her hands. Between her palms, she formed a swirling water sphere. When it got to the size of a basketball, she pushed it toward Keren.

Keren shuffled back until her shoulders pressed against the building. The force of the water sphere crashing against her shield sent pain radiating up her arm.

Her shield would fail soon. She needed her creatures. While closing her eyes, Keren called for the pulse. It sprang to life, eager to be set free. It pounded in a steady rhythm in her solar plexus like a blacksmith hammering steel. She pushed the pulse up her neck, then behind her eyes. Her eyes snapped open as the golden glow of magic engulfed her body.

The security guard staggered back a few steps, stunned by the golden light swirling around Keren.

"Three!" Keren called out to her earth-elemental creature.

Mist swirled behind the fox shifters, then formed into a towering creature. A feline head crowned with a golden mane sat atop a ten-foot-tall grizzly bear body. Oversized canine teeth jutted from Three's jaw. Branches and twigs interwove over its dark green fur.

After Keren's earth-elemental creature released a ferocious growl, both shifters spun around to face their new adversary. The security guard lifted his hands and shot a water jet at Three's head. Using its oversized hand, Three blocked the attack. A force that would normally have shattered cinder blocks looked as harmless as a faucet sprayer against Keren's creature. With a scream of frustration, the security guard clenched his fists and waved them in the air.

The earth-elemental creature stepped back, drawing the shifters away from Keren. As Three moved, it swept its branch-covered hand back and forth along the ground, attempting to draw the shifters into an attack while keeping its other hand up and ready to defend itself.

The woman fox shifter dove forward, her belly flopping onto the ground, and grabbed Three's fingers as its hand swept by her. With Three's arm extending in length as the shifter's body dragged along the ground, its sweeping arm took the security guard's feet out from under him.

The security guard snarled, then kipped back up like a martial arts fighter. He screamed as his face turned a bright scarlet. Then he lunged at Three's chest. Both shifters tore at Three's branch-covered flesh like rabid animals.

Keren dropped her shield and pulled her hand to her chest. She cradled it while trying to move her blackened fingers. The black dots had traveled all the way to her elbow.

"Don't hurt them!" Keren cried out to Three.

Both fox shifters had magic frenzy, a condition brought on by the quick influx of massive amounts of water elemental magic. Keren hadn't realized the horrible consequences she'd released on the fox-shifter race when she'd saved Nadria's life by pulling magic from the elemental realm.

Until she figured out how to cure magic frenzy and bring all the fox shifters back from this crazed state, the best they could do was to restrain the infected shifters.

"Two, Four, we need your help!" Keren shouted.

Mist swirled next to Three, then formed into an imposing shoulder-height black wolf. Two's massive head supported ram horns ablaze with fire. Beside Two, Four appeared. Keren's water-elemental creature had the upper body of a white fox that tapered into an eel's tail. Royal blue covered the tips of its ears, around its eyes, and its underbelly.

Four twirled once in the air, then waved its paws, creating a water vortex that swirled like a miniature tornado. Two shot fireballs at the fox shifters, trying to dislodge the shifters from Three's body.

The second fireball shot blasted the woman fox shifter off Three's hand. Before she could recover from the blow, Three grabbed her and tossed her into the vortex. Four kept her spinning head over heels so the shifter couldn't get her bearings. Then Three grabbed the security guard with both hands, peeled him off its chest, and flung him into the vortex.

Keren let out a breath of relief as she watched the two fox shifters spinning helplessly in the vortex. She turned when she heard footsteps pounding in her direction. Two inquisitors, both wolf shifters, raced toward her.

"Stop!" the taller inquisitor shouted as he held up his palm. "Don't move. Put your hands in the air."

Keren obeyed the command and raised her hands just above her shoulders. She released Three and Two, and they turned to mist and dissipated into the air.

"Frank, it's me," she called out.

Frank stood a foot taller than his partner, Sally. His long, gangly limbs looked awkward next to Sally's lean, compact runner's stride. They both wore traditional inquisitor uniforms of light blue shirts and dark blue pants. When the inquisitors reached Keren, they stared at Four's water vortex.

Frank looked at it warily. "We thought this was some sort of new fox-shifter magic." He slowly dropped his arm to his side.

Keren lowered her hands. "It's Four's magic. You have nothing to worry about." She gestured to the spinning fox shifters. "We should get them back to the station."

"We have to sedate them first," Frank said as he unclipped a pouch from his belt. He looked at Keren. "Can you stop," he pointed at the vortex, "this?"

"Four," Keren looked up at her water-elemental creature. She was grateful magic frenzy hadn't affected Four, although she didn't fully understand why it hadn't. "We need them unconscious."

With a nod, Four waved its hands, causing the vortex to speed up. The magic twirled the fox shifters like a giant mixer. Then Four slowed the vortex and gently laid the unconscious the fox shifters on the ground.

When the inquisitors hesitated to approach, Keren released Four, and the water-elemental creature dissipated into mist.

Frank gave a heavy sigh, then stepped up and sedated both fox shifters. "I'll never get used to those things," he muttered under his breath.

Keren knew her creatures made most shifters uncomfortable, so she ignored his comment. "That makes five we've subdued this morning," she said.

"Yes, it's getting pretty crowded at the station," Sally said.

Keren looked at the bedraggled fox shifters lying helplessly on the ground. Until Keren found a cure, these and hundreds of other fox shifters like them would pile up in holding cells and spend their lives in a deep-sedation state. Her chest clenched as she shook her head. "This won't work long term."

"You're right." Sally shook her head. "This is a world crisis. I heard leaders are meeting to decide how to deal with this horrible magic frenzy." She bent down to check the fox shifters' pulses. Keren noticed her slight hesitation before touching their necks. "The other shifter races are afraid it will happen to them. It's chaos."

Keren swallowed the lump in her throat. Her friends had agreed to keep the fact she had caused magic frenzy in strict confidence in order to keep her free to research how to pull the water magic back and release the fox shifters from this torture. She knew the truth would eventually leak out. She was living on borrowed time.

Keren cradled her injured hand and rolled her head, stretching out her neck muscles. Her shoulders had tight knots, and she knew she was at her limit with sorcerer magic. She'd been working with inquisitors to hunt rogue fox shifters for the last four hours, and it was time she took a break.

She pulled her phone out and checked the time. "I have to go to the hospital to visit my sister."

"We can drop you off," Frank said as he hefted one of the fox shifters over his shoulder.

"I don't want to inconvenience you," Keren said.

"You're not. We appreciate the help." He nodded at her blackened hand. "You should get that checked out while you're there."

Keren pushed her hand into her pocket, hiding her black-tinged fingers. "Thanks. I'm fine." She released her magic and followed the inquisitors to their car.

CHAPTER TWO

KEREN

Frank slowed the police car in front of the hospital and turned to Keren. "You need help to get through that mob?"

Keren looked out her window at the dozens of reporters standing outside the hospital. For safety, the mayor had ordered the evacuation of citizens from Las Vegas when the battles first began. Unfortunately, that order didn't apply to the press.

She turned to Frank. "No, I'll be fine."

"Alright." Frank stopped the car. "So, we'll see you back at the station?"

"Yeah, maybe later today." Keren smiled and said goodbye to both Frank and Sally, then stepped out of the car.

She watched them drive away, then turned toward the hospital. The reporters had already spotted her and were ambling toward her, dragging their audio and video equipment as if they were robotic appendages. Maybe she should have taken Frank up on his offer.

Keren walked with purpose toward the hospital. Then, like in epic war movies where the heroic army battlefront crashes full force into their charging enemy, Keren felt the impact of the reporters as they swarmed around her. While wiggling her way through the throng blocking her path, she kept her eyes down and stayed focused on getting to the hospital's door.

A woman shoved a microphone in her face. "Ms. Stewart, can you tell us about your sister?"

"No comment," Keren muttered as she squirmed past a chubby, twenty-something-year-old man holding a camera on his shoulder.

Another news reporter shouted, "Is it true your sister brought magic frenzy with her from the elemental realm?"

Anger bubbled in Keren's chest. How dare they attack her sister? She whirled around. "No, that's not true." She clenched her fists. "Why can't you just leave us alone?"

That bit of acknowledgment started a chaotic circus of reporters shouting questions and pressing closer. Keren thought she might suffocate if she didn't do something.

She took in a deep breath and then let out as loud of a scream as she could muster. The stunned reporters stopped shouting and stepped back. Using that moment of confusion, Keren raced to the hospital doors.

After finally making it inside, she kept running until the racket of the reporters faded behind her. Then she slowed her pace, letting out a deep sigh and enjoying the peaceful silence. Actually, she felt better. That scream released some of her pent-up tension, like steam escaping from a boiling teapot. I should try that more often, she thought.

Thank goodness inquisitors had restricted the reporters from coming inside the hospital. This was a welcome reprieve from their vexing shouts.

When Keren rounded the corner to the main reception area, the attendant at the information desk gave her a disgusted look. No one enjoyed dealing with the reporters, and everyone knew why they were here.

As Keren walked by, she gave the attendant an unreturned smile. Keren sighed. She couldn't blame the hospital staff. Ever since the media had gotten a hold of the story about Katrina's rescue from the elemental realm, cameras and reporters had been swarming the hospital.

She stepped onto the elevator and hit the blue button, the one for the restricted ward. With concerns a reporter might sneak into the hospital, Keren had insisted Katrina's doctor move her to the restricted ward for extra protection.

Once she'd made it through security checks, Keren headed to her sister's room. When she stopped in front of the room's two large windows, Keren saw Katrina sitting up in bed. She had more color in her face than she'd had during Keren's last visit.

Keren pushed the door open. "Katrina?"

Katrina turned to the door and smiled. Keren still hadn't gotten used to another person looking like her. Their long chestnut hair, full lips, and round faces made them identical twins. Well, except for the eyes. Katrina had golden eyes where hers were silver. But because both were rare eye colors, Keren wasn't sure if their eyes were a genetic trait or caused by the twisted curse.

Keren walked close to the bed but was careful to keep a safe distance. Anyone with elemental magic who touched Katrina had their magic drained, which resulted in death. That included all shifters and Keren.

"Have the doctors figured out a cure? I'd love to give you a hug."

Katrina shook her head while pushing out her lower lip.

Keren sighed. "I'm sure they'll figure out what's wrong any day now."

Katrina held up a finger. She opened her mouth, but just a puff of air came out. She took a deep breath, then tried again.

"Hi." Katrina's voice was raspy but understandable.

"Oh my gosh, hi." Keren smiled. "I knew you could do it." Hearing Katrina's voice after her sister's twenty-year imprisonment in the elemental realm warmed Keren's heart.

Katrina beamed. "Hi," she said again. Keren laughed, and Katrina clapped her hands with excitement.

Katrina waved her hand at a stack of magazines next to the bed.

Keren picked them up. "You want these?"

Katrina nodded her head and reached out her hand. After taking the magazines, Katrina pulled out four pages she had torn from them. One had a picture of a bat, one a picture of a bear, one a picture of a wolf, and one a picture of a fox. She spread the pictures out on her bed and smiled.

Keren frowned as she took a step forward and looked at the pictures. "Are these my creatures?"

Katrina nodded and patted her chest.

"I don't understand," Keren said.

Katrina pointed to the pictures, then patted her chest again. She opened her mouth, but when no words came out, she frowned in frustration.

While tilting her head, Keren tried to work out what Katrina wanted. "You want to see my creatures?"

Katrina picked up the picture of the bat and extended her arm. After pointing to the picture, she pointed to herself. Tears brimmed in Katrina's eyes as she continued to point to the bat, then herself.

Keren wondered how Katrina knew about One. Her sister had seen all of Keren's creatures except for One, her air-elemental creature, during their escape from the dragons' treasure cavern.

"Let me summon One." Keren closed her eyes and searched for the pulse in her solar plexus. It beat with a steady, calm rhythm. She let the pulse slide up her neck to the back of her eyes. When she opened her eyes, her magic shimmered around her skin.

Katrina's face beamed as she continued to point at the bat picture.

"One," Keren said. "I want you to meet my sister, Katrina."

Mist swirled next to Keren, then One appeared. Batlike wings supported a lizard body. A set of razor-sharp teeth and beady, red eyes made One look ferocious. But with Keren, it acted like a jokester. It did a somersault, then playfully snapped its long, thin tail.

Katrina put the picture down, then placed both hands on her chest. One hovered above Keren, looking down at Katrina.

"Do you know One?" Keren asked.

Katrina nodded, then patted her chest. No, thought Keren, Katrina patted her heart.

"Did you interact with my creatures in the elemental realm?" Keren asked.

Katrina nodded as she watched One.

"So, they kept you company? All those years?" Keren pulled a chair over and sat down. This could be important to finding out what had happened to Katrina while she was in the elemental realm. "Did you interact with anything or anyone else?"

Katrina's smile faded and her eyes bore into Keren's, causing Keren's breath to hitch as memories flooded back to her.

Even as a child, Keren had seen the dark, misty cloud with golden eyes looking at her through the shroud between the elemental realm and the earth realm. The chilling sensation she had experienced when the dark cloud found her made Keren push it away. She had thought it was evil when, all along, it had been Katrina reaching out to her.

Keren rubbed the back of her neck, feeling suddenly uncomfortable and wanting to divert the conversation.

"Magic balances. Maybe when the twisted curse gave me elemental magic, it made you the negative. A force that takes magic away." Keren frowned. "But I wonder how you ended up sealed away?"

Katrina shook her head while shrugging her shoulders.

Keren turned when she heard a knock on the door. She frowned, and her chest bubbled with annoyance at seeing Itorn. The wrinkles etched around his eyes and chiseled into his forehead contrasted with his dyed jet-black hair styled into an Elvis pompadour.

Keren and the elder sorcerer had worked through multiple confrontations in the past. He had been in charge of Katrina's care after they had first rescued her from the elemental realm. However, after some questionable testing on her sister and his terrible bedside manner, Keren had banned Itorn from seeing Katrina. She made a mental note to talk to the guards posted at the restricted ward's security point. He waved a hand, motioning for Keren to come out.

With a huff of frustration, Keren said to Katrina, "I'll just be a minute." She walked to the door and stepped into the corridor. "What do you want?" Keren asked in an irritated tone. "You're not supposed to be here."

"I'm here out of courtesy." Itorn scowled at her. "Now I'm thinking maybe you shouldn't know."

Keren hated the manipulation tactics sorcerers used, especially Itorn. But she couldn't help herself from asking, "Know what?"

Itorn crossed his arms, and a smug look appeared on his face. "I've uncovered CIA agents working covertly in the hospital. They've been inquiring about Katrina."

She squinted at Itorn. "What? Why would the CIA be interested in Katrina?"

"They've been asking about her test results." Itorn leaned closer. "Several vials of Katrina's blood are missing."

Keren knew what Itorn was implying by his sinister tone. He knew if Katrina's blood touched someone with elemental magic, it would drain their magic and kill them, just as touching her would. Her sister was the first of her kind with that dreadful power.

She looked back at Katrina through the window. One entertained her with somersaults as her sister laughed and clapped her hands. Keren pursed her lips in determination. No one would ever hurt her sister.

She turned to Itorn. "Are you saying she's not safe here?"

Itorn nodded his head. "I'm certain she's not."

"Then I'm arranging for her release. Right now." Keren put her hand on the doorknob.

Itorn grabbed her shoulder. "Wait. If you make a scene, that might cause an unpleasant reaction with the agents. I have another option."

She looked back at Itron. Of course he had another option. He wouldn't be here unless he had. "What are you proposing?"

"That I secretly take her to a secure location. Where the CIA won't find her."

Keren frowned. Backdoor dealings and mysterious locations were right up Itorn's alley, and Keren wanted no part of it. "No, I can take her to Calypso's."

"No, you can't." Itorn shook his head. "That's the first place they'll look."

He was right. Besides, if she brought Katrina to Calypso's, she would endanger Gabriel and the hatchlings, who had recently become strong enough to leave the nest and spend time at the mansion. "Then she could stay with Briggs."

"Don't be ridiculous." He pointed to his head. "Think, Keren. They know your connection to him. Besides, you'd be risking his career." He put his hand on his chest. "Only I can take her to a secure location."

Keren shook her head. This had to be a paranoid conspiracy theory. "No. Katrina's not a criminal or anyone's prisoner. She can go wherever she pleases."

"Don't be so sure." Itorn lowered his voice. "I've heard murmurs of protective custody."

"Protection from whom?" Keren asked in a too-loud voice that startled even herself.

Keren looked through the window. Katrina was staring at her with a baffled look on her face. Keren gave her a smile and a thumbs up, then turned back to Itorn.

He spoke in a hushed tone. "I think *protective custody* is just a government double-talk ruse. They think she's a threat. Once the government has her, you'll never see her again."

Keren's chest tightened around her pounding heart. She'd just rescued her sister, and it was her job to keep Katrina safe. Itorn was a powerful sorcerer, and Keren couldn't deny his cleverness for discerning threatening situations. If she had to overlook her personal feelings toward him to keep Katrina safe, then so be it. In a whisper, she said, "Let me hear your plan."

"First, we need my trusted colleague who is waiting nearby," Itorn said.

Keren frowned. "Against human CIA agents? The two of us can handle them."

"How far are you willing to go?" Itorn asked. "Are you willing to kill?" He paused, glaring at Keren. "I'm not. I represent all sorcerers, and I won't turn them all into wanted criminals to save your sister."

Keren blinked. The last thing she wanted was anyone else to get hurt. "So, why are you here?"

"To get Katrina to a secure location, without bloodshed, before the government acts and she disappears forever." He held up his phone. "My colleague is waiting for my instructions. What's your decision?"

The thought of Katrina being alone with sorcerers she didn't know made Keren's stomach clench. She wouldn't wish that on her worst enemy. "No way," Keren blurted. "I'm not leaving Katrina with strangers. Especially not sorcerers."

"It's your best chance to keep her safe. I have contacts across the world that can help her fall off the radar."

Keren took a step back. "I don't want my sister to fall off the radar."

"I think you do. At least for now," Itorn said. "It's us or the government."

Keren pursed her lips. If she hadn't needed to find a cure for magic frenzy, Keren would disappear with Katrina herself.

"Maybe protective custody isn't a bad thing." She glanced back at Katrina playing with One. Katrina knew nothing about the world. Someone would have to look out for her 24/7 once the doctor discharged her from the hospital. Until they identified whatever illness Katrina had, she couldn't stay with shifters because of the danger she posed to them.

Itorn's prophetic whispers floated into Keren's ear. "You'd never see her again. The government will whisk her away, and it will be like Katrina never existed." Itorn glanced at Katrina, then back at Keren. "Are you willing to let her go so easily?"

"You can't know that," Keren said. Itorn's insistence and irritating voice were giving her a headache. "I don't see her being held by the government or by you sorcerers much differently."

Itorn raised his eyebrows. "*We* sorcerers..."

Keren rolled her eyes, and Itorn grabbed her arm.

"Yes, we sorcerers, you included, band together and help one another. Whether you like it or not, you are a sorcerer." He pointed at Katrina. "And most likely, so is your twin sister." His eyes drilled into Keren's. "Are you willing to turn your sister over to an agency with misguided beliefs about magic? What do you think they will do with her? Don't let our past cloud your decision." He bent closer. "Trust me. Let me keep her safe."

Keren stepped back. She might not like Itorn, but she knew him. She knew him to be impertinent and condescending. But she also knew him to be extremely protective of his people. Trusting the government was a wild card. Keren rubbed her temples, disbelieving what she was about to say.

"You'll let me know where you're at?" she asked. "I don't plan on abandoning my sister."

Itorn frowned. "I'm not sure that's a good idea. If you're interrogated, it's better if you don't know."

She tried to protest, but he hushed her when two men in suits turned the corner.

The taller man sported the dad-bod look. He might have been athletic in his younger years, but a too-busy, middle-aged life had awarded him with a modest "beer belly." The shorter man's bald head glistened under the florescent lighting. The way his arm muscles punched against his jacket sleeves made Keren think he might be a bodybuilder. The men chatted as they paused at the windows to Katrina's room.

"Is this her room?" the taller of the two men asked.

"Yes," the other one answered. Then he looked at Keren and Itorn. "I'm sorry, we didn't mean to interrupt." He smiled as his eyes gazed at the golden glow flowing over Keren's skin. "You must be Keren. I've read a great deal about you. I'm Ray Gibson."

"Yes," Keren said, tentatively taking Ray's extended hand. "I'm sorry, but my sister isn't taking visitors."

"Oh." His chest deflated with disappointment. "Maybe another time." He turned to the taller man. "We'll discuss the details in my office." He smiled at Keren. "It was nice meeting you." Then they turned and walked away.

After the men were far enough away to not overhear them, Itorn turned to Keren. "Do you see? Decide, or they will decide for you."

Keren sighed. Those must the CIA agents Itorn had spoken of. "Why can't they just leave Katrina alone?" She looked at her sister, who was laughing at One. "It's not really my decision."

Itorn frowned. "What do you mean?"

"My sister's an adult. She has a mind of her own. I think she should decide."

Itorn snorted. "How can she understand the gravity of the situation?"

Keren nodded. "We'll have to help her understand." She looked at Itorn. "Let's go."

With that, Keren walked back into Katrina's room, and Itorn followed behind.

"Katrina," she said. "Itorn and I have something to discuss with you."

Katrina's face darkened as her body stiffened. Apparently, she felt the same way about the elder sorcerer as Keren.

"Relax." Keren held her hands out. "I brought Itorn in to talk about something important." Keren turned to Itorn. "Why don't you explain?"

"CIA agents are looking to take you into protective custody, where they may hold you for the rest of your life. I'm offering to provide a haven to prevent you from falling into the government's hands."

Katrina grabbed her blankets and squeezed so tight her knuckles turned white. She had a confused and frightened look on her face. Keren rubbed her forehead. That was a truthful but brutal explanation.

She sat on the bed, careful not to touch Katrina. "Let me try to explain." She looked down to gather her thoughts. Then she looked at Katrina and spoke in a calming tone. "Please don't think all government agents are bad. They protect our country. With that said, sometimes people ... well ... disappear when the government gets involved. Protective custody isn't what we want for you." She hesitated, then continued. "We're afraid we might not get you back."

Katrina's face turned from worried to petrified.

Tears brimmed in Keren's eyes. This was the last thing her sister needed. After all she'd been through, she deserved a safe, happy life.

"We don't want to tip them off. So we'll have to think of a plan to sneak you out of the hospital," Keren said.

Katrina pointed at Keren.

"No." Keren shook her head as she brushed a tear away. "I can't come with you right now. But I'll join you as soon as I can. This will be temporary."

"The government never stops," Itorn said. "You're talking like they will simply throw up their hands and give up."

Keren balled her hands into fists and spoke to Itorn through clenched teeth. "I'm not abandoning my sister."

Itorn's muscles tensed, then he quickly gained his composure. "Fine. Once she's settled, we'll send for you."

Hearing voices in the hall, everyone turned. The two men were standing outside again. The tall one was talking while the other was nodding his head. They didn't seem to care that they were being watched. The glass made it impossible to understand their conversation, but Keren could only imagine what they were saying.

Itorn turned to Keren and Katrina and spoke in a low tone. "We should move now."

"Now?" Keren said.

Katrina tugged at her blankets. She nodded as if she were saying she wanted to go ahead with the plan.

"They suspect something," Itorn said. "We must move now."

Keren ran through her options. Having Katrina walk out in a hospital gown wouldn't work.

"I'll trade places with her," Keren said.

"What?" Itorn asked.

"I'll swap clothes with her, and you two can walk out. Everyone will think it's me."

Itorn rubbed his chin. "That could work. We'll have to work around the regular nurse visits."

Katrina shook her head and frowned.

Keren smiled at her sister. "I'll be fine. What matters is getting you out."

"It's risky," Itorn said. He pulled out his phone. "But it could work. I'll update my colleague with the plan."

"It's alright," Keren said, trying to sooth her sister's fear. "I'll join you shortly."

Katrina bit her lip, then nodded.

"Then it's settled," Itorn said. "After the next nurse's visit, you'll switch places."

Keren stood and stepped up to Itorn. "Tell me when she's safe and exactly where she's at." She poked a finger at his chest. "I mean it."

"It will be difficult," Itorn said. "You know the government will have us all under surveillance."

Keren stepped closer to him and spoke in a commanding tone. "Promise me you'll let me know when she's safe and where she's located. That's the only way I'll agree."

"I'll get word to you. I promise." Itorn stepped back and typed another message into his phone.

Keren stared at Itorn. Was this churning in her gut because of him or the CIA agents? She shook off the feeling. Everything will be fine, she told herself. This was best for Katrina.

Keren ran her fingers through her hair. "What will I wear out of the hospital? How long should I stay before I leave?"

"I'll get you scrubs," Itorn said.

Keren's chest tightened. She had worn scrubs to sneak into the hospital to visit her mom after the inquisitors restricted her visits. That was right after the magic attack that almost killed her mom, and it was a time Keren would prefer to forget.

She swallowed down her trepidation. "How long do I have to impersonate Katrina for?"

"Four or maybe five hours," Itorn said. "That and the time it will take for the agents to figure out what happened will give us enough time to get out of the city."

Four hours, Keren thought. How would she fool the nurses for so long?

"I'll have to be hooked up to the heart rate monitor." Keren's eyes wandered to the tube snaking out of Katrina's arm. "And you'll have to hook me up to Katrina's IV." Keren poked at the bag. "What's in here?"

Itorn reached for Katrina's chart. "It's saline, for the dehydration. It won't hurt you. You can close the valve after the nurse leaves."

"Then it's decided," Keren said with a nod, trying to boost her own confidence. "After the next nurse check-in, we'll switch places. And, Itorn, you'll take Katrina safely away."

Still, something didn't sit well with Keren. Had they overlooked a detail? It would be easy to rush into this plan. She released her magic and prepared for the switch.

Keren sat in the hospital bed, waiting for the half-hour mark. Then she'd turn on the IV valve and pretend to be asleep. She didn't want the nurse seeing her eyes.

Katrina, who had put on Keren's clothes, left with Itorn twenty minutes ago. Not knowing if they had made it out and if Katrina was safe rattled Keren's nerves.

"You can do this," she told herself.

When she heard voices in the hall, her mind raced. At the window stood the two CIA agents. Seeing her alone, Ray Gibson opened the door.

"Excuse me," he said. "Do you mind if we come in? Mr. Halloway would like to meet you."

Keren stared at them, unsure what to do. Maybe she could get some information from them. She waved them in. Crap, she'd have to remember she wasn't supposed to talk.

"Thank you," Ray said. "Let me introduce myself. I'm Ray Gibson, the president of Sunrise Hospital. I've held my position for fifteen years."

Goose bumps quivered on Keren's skin. The CIA has had control over the hospital for fifteen years?

Ray continued. "I'm giving a potential investor a tour, and he'd very much like to meet you."

The taller man stepped forward and extended his hand. "I'm Peter. I've read so much about you."

As she tried not to let her jaw drop, Keren shook his hand.

"You're a celebrity in the eyes of my daughter. She's fascinated with magic and dreams of being part of the magic races." He shuffled nervously. "Can I get a selfie with you?"

What CIA agent wants a selfie? This was taking "undercover" a bit too far.

She had to find out more. To heck with not being able to speak. "You said you're an investor?" Keren asked as she leaned her head toward Peter.

Peter held his phone up in front of their faces and snapped a couple of pictures. "Yes. Sunrise's advanced research on treating magic races has helped the entire world save lives." He checked the selfie on his phone and smiled. "My daughter will love this." He tapped a few keys, then put his phone in his pocket.

"So, you're not a CIA agent?" Keren asked.

The man laughed. "Heavens no. What made you think that?"

Anger boiled in her chest. Itorn had deceived her. "Just ... someone told me you were."

The man reached into his pocket and pulled out his ID. "I'm not sure who would tell you that." He patted his belly and held the ID out to Keren. "I'm sure the CIA wouldn't allow me through their doors. You have nothing to worry about."

Keren leaned forward and read the ID. *Peter Halloway*, it said.

The president picked up Katrina's file. "Miss Stewart, it says here you're nontalking." His face lit up. "Let me get the doctors. This is a wonderful breakthrough."

"Yeah," Keren said as her head spun. Her words were lackluster. "It's a miracle."

"I'll send the doctor right in." He put her chart back. "Please come with me, Mr. Halloway. Ms. Stewart needs her rest."

"Thanks again," Peter said as he waved, then followed Ray toward the door.

After the men left, Keren jumped from the bed. She pulled out the scrubs she'd hidden under the mattress. After tugging them on over her hospital gown, she yanked the IV out of her arm, oblivious to the pain.

"Itorn," she growled. "Just wait until I get my hands on you."

She grabbed Katrina's chart, then bolted from the room and ran down the corridor. Thankfully, there was no sign of Ray or Peter.

Finding the elevator too slow, she burst into the stairwell and took two stairs at a time until she reached the ground floor. Pulling her phone out, she cursed at letting Itorn get the better of her. She searched the hospital lobby but saw no signs of Itorn or Katrina.

"Hello?" Gaines said.

"Gaines, it's Keren." She raced through the hospital lobby and out the front door. Like ants to sugar, the reporters scurried after her, but she ignored them. Her words came out between panting breaths. "I need you at Sunrise Hospital."

"Sure," he said. "What's the emergency? Do I need to bring backup?"

Keren skidded to a stop in the parking lot. Gaines had always said the Puca Investigation Bureau, PIB for short, knew what others didn't. She prayed he was right.

"I need your agents to find Itorn. He kidnapped Katrina." The words sent a quake through her body.

"How could he have kidnapped her? Or why?"

"I'll explain when you get here. Please hurry." Keren scrubbed a hand through her hair. She felt humiliated. Itorn's story about government agents had totally duped her. Now he had Katrina's life in his hands.

"I'm on my way," Gaines said.

Tension built as she searched the sky for Gaines. The reporters' questions buzzed like bees in a blur around her. She dialed Briggs's number. When the phone went to voice mail after several rings, she swore. "Where are you, Briggs?" After the away message, she asked him to call her back right away.

She waved her arms in the air when she spotted Gaines. The reporters backed away a few steps when a sleek, black dragon swooped down and made a gentle landing in the parking lot. His sharp talons dug into the asphalt as though it were sand.

The puca's dragon form was smaller than that of a real dragon, but no less impressive. Gaines's wings folded into his body, and his long neck retracted as he transformed into his human form. Once the transformation completed, the puca stood five feet tall. His loose-fitting jeans and T-shirt gave him a preppy, college look.

He ran up to Keren, his horse ears perking forward as he scanned the parking lot. Holding up his PIB badge, he shouted to the reporters, "Step back." He pointed at them. "Further back."

Grumbling protests, the reporters did as Gaines ordered.

Once they were far enough away, he turned to Keren. "What happened?" he asked. "I thought you banned Itorn from seeing Katrina."

"I did." Keren spat out. "But he came to me with a wild story about government agents being in the hospital and looking to put Katrina under protective custody."

Gaines frowned. "That is a wild story. And you believed him?"

Heat rose in Keren's cheeks. "I did because there were two men in suits hanging around outside Katrina's room." She shook her head. "He tricked me into letting him walk right out of the hospital with her."

Gaines whistled. "Ballsy. What do you think he wants with her?"

Keren's heart sank. She had her suspicions. But there was no need to cause a panic. Not yet. "I'm not sure."

Gaines typed on his phone. "I'm engaging two agents. They're two of my best." He looked up at her. "Did he mention where he was going?" He frowned, then shouted at a reporter who had shuffled closer. "I said back up, or I'll arrest you!"

Keren clenched her jaw, thinking about her conversation with Itorn. How could she have been so gullible?

"He said something about a colleague," she said. "A sorcerer he knew that was supposed to move her to a safe location."

"No other information?" Gaines asked.

By the look on his face, Keren knew he thought her a fool for falling for Itorn's story. But he hadn't been there. Everything had happened so quickly.

She shook her head. "Itorn said he'd contact me when Katrina was safe." She felt her face flush with heat. "I'm sure that was another lie."

"How long of a head start does he have?" Gaines asked.

She'd had one nursing visit and had been preparing for the second when the men came into her room. "About an hour."

"I'll have agents contact our sorcerer informants." He typed on the phone. "We have strong relationships. Maybe one of them has an idea of where Itorn might be headed or why he wants Katrina." When he finished, he looked at Keren. "Where can I take you?"

"Calypso's." Keren's head pounded.

CHAPTER THREE

KEREN

Gaines put a hand on Keren's shoulder. "Hang in there. The PIB is on this."

Keren nodded. "Thanks." She held back tears. How could she have let her sister fall into Itorn's hands?

Gaines stepped back and transformed into his dragon form. Keren climbed onto his back and wriggled her hands under his scales to hang on.

When he jumped into the air, Keren looked at what remained of Las Vegas. The Venetian Resort was a pile of rubble. While the STRAT, with its top few floors demolished to make room for the dragons' nest, loomed in the distance. The normally busy streets resembled a war zone with overturned cars and charred streets from the magic battles.

Her phone rang. Maybe it was Briggs. She pressed her chest against Gaines's neck so she could wiggle her phone out of her pocket. Disappointment passed through her when the caller ID showed Theodore Hopkins.

She answered the phone. "Hello? Theodore? Do you have any word on my mom?"

"Yes. Is now a good time?" Theodore asked.

A gust of wind almost blew her phone from her hand. Although she felt she couldn't deal with anything else right now, she knew she couldn't ignore her efforts to get her mom paroled from prison. "No, but you can come over to Calypso's. I'm on my way there."

"I'll meet you there. See you in about half an hour." Theodore hung up.

As Gaines banked toward Calypso's mansion, Keren's heart pounded, hoping she was wrong about Itorn's intentions. She hoped Calypso would help with the search.

After Gaines landed in front of Calypso's and Keren slid off his back, he changed into his human form.

Keren pulled out her phone. No messages from Briggs. She called him again. No answer. An uneasy feeling churned in her gut.

"Will you go in with me?" Keren asked. She would need at least one ally when she faced Calypso.

"Yeah." Gaines smiled and motioned Keren to the door. "I'd be happy to."

Keren lifted the door knocker, then paused. She'd moved into Calypso's last week after being invited. To her, that meant she shouldn't have to knock. She reached down and turned the handle, then walked in.

"Calypso?" Keren shouted.

Her voice echoed in the high-ceilinged, extravagant foyer. Her shoes squeaked as she walked across the custom Italian tile toward the drawing room. She hesitated as she rested her hand on the door handle. Before she could turn it, the door opened. Ryota's slender, muscular frame blocked the doorway. He wore his herringbone newsboy hat tipped slightly to the side.

His disapproving eyes looked at Keren. "You invited yourself in."

She didn't care what this dragon thought of her. She officially lived here and had a right to come and go as she pleased.

Keren pushed past Ryota, with Gaines following behind. "I live here, remember?"

Drawing room was Calypso's code word for his personal bar and entertainment room. A high-end, restaurant-style bar took up one wall of the room. Wine glasses, martini glasses, and shot and rocks glasses shimmered on the racks and hangers. On the back wall of the bar were high-end, expensive liquors of all varieties. A luxurious linen couch and two oversized chairs sat to the side, surrounding a handmade mahogany coffee table.

Calypso stood at the bar. His blue polo shirt showed off his taut, muscular arms. Stylishly slicked back, white hair and a six-foot, lean build completed Calypso's high-end male-model look. Gabriel, his mate, sat on a barstool by his side. A leather pencil skirt and a sheer blouse with a deep neckline showed off Gabriel's curves. Her luxurious, glossy black hair cascaded past the barstool. Calypso's world revolved around Gabriel and his children. He leaned into Gabriel, as if he couldn't get close enough.

Calypso glanced at Keren, then refocused on Gabriel. "Hello, Keren. You seem upset," he said as he stroked Gabriel's silky hair. "Having problems with your fox-shifter hunt?"

Keren's throat tightened, knowing she'd let her family down again.

"Itorn took Katrina," she said.

Calypso raised an eyebrow as he turned his attention to Keren. "Did he?"

Gabriel ran a hand across Calypso's square jawline. "I'll leave you to your business dealings. I'll take the hatchlings back to the nest." Her lips brushed over his. "Join us when you're finished."

Calypso kissed Gabriel's hand. "I won't be long, my love."

Gabriel walked up to Keren. Her vibrant blue-green eyes sparkled. "It's nice to see you again," she said as she passed by.

Keren gave Gabriel a weak smile. "Likewise."

She waited for Gabriel to close the door before she faced Calypso and blurted out, "Itorn duped me. He said there were CIA agents looking to put Katrina in protective custody." Keren paced the floor and ran her fingers through her hair. "It was all a bluff. He said he was protecting her. But he lied. Those men weren't agents. Itorn wanted Katrina."

"What men?" Calypso asked.

"Two men in suits were hanging around Katrina's room. Itorn said they were CIA, but they were really the hospital president and an investor."

Calypso's eyes narrowed. "Itorn's intent for Katrina can't be good."

"No," Keren said. "I think it will be detrimental to all shifters."

"How can kidnapping Katrina be detrimental to shifters?" Gaines asked.

Keren turned to Gaines. "When Katrina touches a shifter, she drains their magic."

"How can that happen?" Gaines asked, looking confused.

"No one knows," Keren said. "The doctors were running tests to determine what exactly was different about her blood."

Blood. Keren's eyes widened. Oh no. Itorn had said someone had stolen several vials of Katrina's blood. She held up Katrina's chart. "I grabbed this when I left the hospital. Maybe it has information we can use."

Gaines took the chart. "I'll have an agent pull the electronic records." His phone buzzed, and he took the call. "Yes, I see." He looked at Keren, then

Calypso. "You need to hear this." He pressed the speakerphone button. "Repeat what you just said."

The words coming from the phone sent chills down Keren's spine: "We've found a report of three shifters killed under suspicious circumstances. Something drained their magic."

"Fox shifters?" Gaines asked, his eyes showing worry and concern.

"One fox shifter," the voice replied. "But two wolf shifters. Someone used a dart gun on them. We're following up on leads."

Gaines took the phone off speaker. "Good work. I need you to pull all the medical information you can find on Katrina Stewart." He nodded. "Yes, that's right. Keep me updated." Then he hung up.

"No. This is a calamity." The words rumbled out of Calypso's mouth like thunder. He pushed himself away from the bar. "He's weaponizing her."

"Weaponizing?" Gaines asked. "How?"

Keren's heart pounded. She hated to admit it, but she knew Calypso was right.

"Her blood," she said. She flipped through Katrina's chart. "Here." A shaky finger pointed to the page. "Any contact with her blood has the same results as her touch."

The room went silent. Itorn planned to use Katrina as a blood bank to power an attack against shifters.

"We have to stop him," Keren said.

"You can't stop this," Calypso said. "If it's not Itorn, it will be another greedy sorcerer or human wanting to eliminate the shifter races." His face darkened. "You might not want to face it, but the only way to stop this is to eliminate your sister."

"No!" Keren shouted. On instinct, she reached for the pulse. It pounded in her solar plexus, begging to be set free.

"There is no cure," Calypso said as he pointed a finger at Keren. "Just like there is no cure for you." He squinted and tipped his head. "I know you're fighting the urge to call on your creatures. Calm down and remember that I am not your enemy."

Keren let out a heavy sigh. She released the pulse. Calypso was right. He wasn't her enemy. But that didn't stop his words from cutting her like a knife. "We weren't born this way," Keren said.

"No. Dirty sorcerer magic tainted you." Calypso spat out the words.

You're an abomination. The words echoed in Keren's head. How many times had others said that about her? They were right. In a desperate effort to save her baby girls from the Dark Guild, her mom had cast a twisted curse upon them, making them into the unnatural beings they were today.

Then a thought came to Keren's mind. Wide-eyed, she looked at Calypso. "The twisted curse," she said.

"Yes, that's what I said. The twisted curse created you."

"What if the curse were reversed? Like we're planning to do for Jewel?"

Calypso frowned. "Interesting proposal." He drummed his fingers on the bar as he took a moment to contemplate. "You don't know if a spell like that would kill you or cure you. Are you willing to take the risk?"

"Once word gets out that Katrina's blood is being used to target shifters, she'll be on everyone's hit list. At least trying to reverse the twisted curse gives us a chance."

Keren jumped when the door slammed open.

CHAPTER FOUR

KEREN

Sirena stomped into the drawing room wearing a light-blue empire-cut dress. White lace embroidered with small red flowers adorned the deep V-shaped neckline. Long sleeves billowing down her arms with tight lace cuffs just above the elbows made the mermaid look like a princess from a medieval story.

She'd twisted her crimson locks into a loose swirl on top of her head, exposing her elven ears she'd inherited from her mom. An emerald clip kept the hair in place, just as it had when Keren first met her.

General Zaim, from the elven army, marched in behind her. The high-powered compound bow strapped to his back and long sword at his side always made Keren feel uneasy.

In one arm, Sirena cradled an egg-shaped vessel containing a glowing, swirling mist. The mist was Jewel, a Chinese dragon who'd been cursed by a sorcerer over a hundred years ago. Sirena's other slender hand rested protectively on the vessel.

Keren's eyes locked onto the golden ring on Sirena's finger. The swooping eagle, a symbol of the elven ruler, was discernible even from this distance.

"Doesn't anyone knock anymore?" Calypso pulled out a barstool and sat. "This is my home, not a hotel."

Ryota pushed in behind the general. "I'm sorry, sir." He gave Sirena a scowl. "I will lock the door from now on."

"Sirena," Keren said. "Now's not the best time."

Sirena walked up to Keren, her blue eyes hard with anger. "Jewel's suffering." She rubbed a hand over the egg-shaped vessel. "When will you lift her curse?"

Already born into merfolk royalty, Sirena's princess status expanded to the elves after the Elf Prince transferred the ring of power to her upon his death. The round-faced teenager had no problem with flexing her elven army's strength to get what she wanted. Right now, she wanted Jewel's curse reversed.

Keren's growing headache felt as though an ice pick were chipping away at her brain. She couldn't deal with Sirena's tantrum right now. With Katrina missing, everything else took a lower priority.

"I told you my mom will help Jewel. But first we have to arrange for her release from prison." Keren looked at her phone. There were no other messages from Theodore. "Her lawyer should be here any minute."

Sirena squinted. "Are you sure your mom can help Jewel?"

"Mom knows more about curses than any other sorcerer I know," Keren said. She stopped herself before saying, "Except for Quinlin Turner," the notorious and insane Dark Guild leader. Just thinking about him made her stomach churn. Thank goodness the judge had sentenced him to life in prison without a chance for parole. "She'll do everything she can."

Sirena lifted her chin. "I shouldn't have to remind you what will happen if any harm comes to Jewel."

Keren rubbed her temple. No, Sirena had given her the "consequences" speech so many times she had regular nightmares about it.

Gaines pointed at the vessel. "Are you communicating with Jewel? That's impressive."

While frowning, Sirena tightened her grip on Jewel. "I'm a mermaid. Jewel is a Chinese dragon. She controls all the seas. Being a mermaid, I can communicate with her." Her hand rubbed over the vessel. "Even in this form."

Gaines smiled. "Nice."

"Don't, Gaines," Keren said.

But Gaines ignored the warning. "So, if something happens to Jewel," he held up both palms, "which, of course, it won't. What will happen?"

In as commanding of a voice as the teenaged mermaid could manage, Sirena said, "If someone harms Jewel, or if she's not released soon from the curse, the merfolk will avenge her by waging war on sorcerers."

Gaines raised his eyebrows as he took a step back. "A war?"

"I told you," Keren whispered to him as she shook her head.

Sirena continued in a louder voice, "As a mermaid, I would join the war against sorcerers with my elven army. We wouldn't stop until we'd killed every sorcerer."

When Sirena finished, the room fell quiet.

Gaines cleared his throat. "Ok. Um. Thanks for the information."

Keren reached out and put a hand on Sirena's arm. "I'm dealing with a lot right now. Trust me. I won't let anything happen to Jewel."

General Zaim's body stiffened, and he stepped closer to Sirena. He didn't like anyone touching her. Too bad. The girl needed reassurance. Keren moved closer and put her arm around Sirena.

"Tell that to my father. He's gathering the merfolk now to prepare for war." She wrinkled her forehead. "He's growing impatient with me. That's what I came to tell you."

A chill ran through Keren's body. "Don't worry," she said. "I'll make this right. I promise."

While blinking back tears, Sirena looked into Keren's eyes, letting her insecurities leak through. She flicked Keren's elf ear with her finger and smiled.

Once when Keren had needed to blend in to an elven crowd, Sirena had manipulated Keren's essence to give her elf ears. Keren had kept them, since having elf ears helped Sirena feel connected to her. They weren't so bad.

Sirena let out a soft laugh. "Sister promise."

Keren smiled. "Sister promise." Then she pulled Sirena into a hug.

Keren turned when she heard Ryota's voice. He stood in the doorway with Theodore at his side.

"Mr. Theodore Hopkins is here to see Keren."

"How many more people have you invited?" Calypso asked.

"I'm sorry. It was a last-minute thing. He's here to talk about my mom's parole," Keren said.

Calypso stood, studying the newcomer. "A sorcerer?" His voice growled. "I thought your mother had a shifter lawyer."

"She does. Or she did," Keren said. "He's a fox shifter." Keren felt a wave of guilt. "He's not available right now."

Calypso grunted. "You mean he has magic frenzy."

Keren gritted her teeth but didn't respond.

The tall sorcerer stepped into the room. His tailored, light-gray suit jacket showed off his wide shoulders and chest. He held a briefcase in one hand.

Sirena stepped up to Theodore. "Are they releasing Keren's mom?"

Keren moved between them. "Theodore, this is Sirena. Sirena, Theodore."

"It's nice to meet you, Sirena." Theodore held out his hand.

When Sirena didn't move, Keren bumped Sirena's shoulder and whispered out the side of her mouth, "He's here to help us."

Sirena lifted her chin. "You didn't answer my question."

The air in the room grew thick, and General Zaim stepped forward. "Answer the Elf Princess."

"I'll have none of that in my home," Calypso bellowed so loud the bar glasses clanked together. "Ryota, show General Zaim outside."

"General," Ryota said, motioning to the door.

After Sirena waved her hand at the general, he scowled but followed Ryota out of the room.

Sirena turned back to Theodore, stretched herself to appear as tall as possible, and lifted her chin. She sucked in her cheeks to look more intimidating. Keren shook her head. This look needed more work.

Gaines took Theodore's hand. "I'm Gaines. Head of the PIB."

"Nice to meet you, Gaines." Theodore nodded at Sirena. "And you, Your Royal Highness." He walked to the bar. "I hope I'm not interrupting." After setting his briefcase on the bar, he released the latches, opened the top, and looked around the room. "Should we go someplace more private?"

"It's fine," Keren said. She figured letting Theodore tell everyone would be faster. She couldn't wait to search for Itorn and get Katrina back. "They are all interested parties."

"Are they releasing Keren's mom?" Sirena asked again.

"That's not a yes or no answer." Theodore pointed to his briefcase. "If you'll allow me to show you the related documents, I can explain where we're at and what comes next."

Keren sat next to Theodore, while Sirena moved to stand next to Keren.

"What have you found?" Keren asked.

Theodore cleared his throat. "I believe we have a strong case." He pulled out a stack of bundled papers. He held one bundle out to Sirena. "Here's a copy if you'd like to follow along. I brought a few extras."

When   she   didn't   move   from   her pouty-teenager-with-way-too-much-power stance, Theodore set the papers on the bar. He handed a bundle to Keren.

Keren picked up the papers and read the first page. "They've scheduled her parole hearing?"

"Yes. The hearing wasn't due until next year." A smile lit up his handsome face. "But because of her good behavior and cooperation in Dark Guild members' trials, they agreed to my petition and moved up the date."

"That's great," Keren said as she flipped through the stack. "What are the chances they'll release her?"

Theodore shrugged. "It's hard to say. If you look at page three, you can see I'm also using the argument for cruel and unusual punishment."

After turning to that page, Keren skimmed the notes. "You think, because of the extensive fear against sorcerers that the Dark Guild created, they gave Mom an unfair sentence?"

"Yes. There's no precedent for a five-year sentence for similar crimes." He rubbed the back of his neck. "It's a long shot since she admitted to joining the Dark Guild in her twenties. But we need all the ammunition we can muster to get her paroled early."

Keren turned the page and frowned. "It says here I'm giving testimony."

"Yes. You must give your testimony as to why your mother deserves to be released and how she isn't a menace to society."

"But the hearing is tomorrow afternoon," Keren said. "I have nothing prepared."

"I'll help you. The judge only signed the call for an emergency hearing a few hours ago." He pressed his fingertips into the bar and furrowed his brows. "It's important you don't talk about why you need her released."

"Why?" Sirena asked. "She's going to release Jewel. What's more important than that?"

Theodore sighed. "I get it. I do." He closed and latched his briefcase. "But we're asking for the release of an incarcerated felon who used deadly force with magic. Telling the parole board you want her released to reverse an unknown curse on an unknown Chinese dragon with unknown power and unknown intentions won't get the results you're looking for. I guarantee it."

Sirena looked at Jewel. "It would if they knew the pain Jewel is going through."

"Sirena, I don't recommend mentioning Jewel at all." Theodore looked at Keren as if asking her what to do.

"I'm going with you." Sirena squeezed Jewel against her chest. "I'll convince them to release your mom."

"That's not a good idea," Keren said.

"Why not?" Calypso asked as he stepped behind the bar. "The Elf Princess can use her amazing charm to persuade the parole board." He gave Keren a wry smile.

"You're not helping," Keren said to Calypso. Then she turned to Sirena and placed a hand on the mermaid's shoulder. "Sirena, you said you trusted me."

Sirena frowned as she pursed her lips. This girl could be so stubborn.

Keren squeezed her shoulder. "I sister promised, right?"

Sirena blinked to fight back tears as she nodded.

Keren smiled. "Good. Let Theodore and me handle this. I'll let you know what happened as soon as the hearing ends."

With a huff, Sirena rolled her eyes. "Fine."

Keren worried about Sirena. Her father had sheltered her all her life. Sirena's experience was nowhere near what it should be at age sixteen. Her father pressured her to be a perfect daughter, and now she was the Elf Princess and had an entire magic race depending on her for their very survival.

"I have time to help you with your testimonial statement." Theodore looked around the room. "Are you sure you don't want to go somewhere more private?"

"Now?" Keren asked. "I'm in the middle of something."

Theodore frowned. "I called in favors to get this parole hearing. We have to have all *t*'s crossed and *i*'s dotted."

"Can we do this tomorrow?" Keren asked.

Theodore shook his head. "We should at least get the draft done tonight. You can practice in the car tomorrow on the way to the hearing."

Keren sighed and rubbed the back of her neck. Her head felt like it would explode at any minute. She looked at Gaines. "Find me if you get any new information."

Gaines gave her a one-finger salute. "Absolutely."

Keren sighed and turned to Theodore. "OK, we can use my room."

"Wait!" Sirena shouted. "You should work here."

Keren fought to keep from screaming at the top of her lungs. She cared about Sirena, she really did. But sometimes the girl was so frustrating. Keren turned to Sirena. "There are too many distractions here. We need privacy." She patted Sirena's arm. "Take care of Jewel."

With that, Keren walked toward the door. She looked at Theodore and motioned with her head for him to follow.

Once they were out of the room and a safe distance away, Theodore let out a sigh. "Wow, she's intense."

"She's young," Keren said. "She's obsessed with freeing Jewel."

Theodore ran a hand through his hair. "You know I can't guarantee the outcome of the parole hearing."

Keren led Theodore up the winding staircase. She opened her bedroom door, which was a little way from the landing, and motioned for him to step inside. "I know." She pulled out her phone and tried Briggs again. No answer. She sighed and followed Theodore into the room.

The expansive bedroom had a king-sized bed on one side with a white four-poster king-sized bed. The bed looked as if it were losing a fight with a throng of eclectic pillows. On the other side of the room were two queen tiffany throne chairs. The teal velvet with gold trim chairs faced a white marble French Victorian-style fireplace. Carvings of flowers, scrolls, and classic acanthus adorned the sides and front. A circular glass coffee table sat between the two chairs.

Theodore set his briefcase on the table. "What will you do if the parole board refuses our request?"

"I'll find another way," Keren said. "There's always another way." She pursed her lips. She would find Itorn and Katrina.

"I wish all my clients were as determined and positive as you." He paused. "Why me?"

Keren frowned. "Why you?"

"Yes. Why pick me as your representative? You know I'm Quinlin Turner's attorney."

"I know," Keren said, lowering her head. She felt guilty for reaching out to the firm representing Quinlin. With Sirena threatening to unleash the elven army if Keren didn't reverse Jewel's curse, Keren had no choice but to use every resource available to get her mom out of prison. "Your law firm is famous for defending magic-race clients."

Theodore leaned back. "I'm assuming Calypso is funding my retainer."

Keren nodded. A hundred years ago, Calypso's brother, Dresdin, had loved Jewel and endlessly searched for the sorcerer who had cursed her. But an elf murdered Dresdin and kidnapped Jewel. Calypso felt an obligation to finish what his brother had started.

"Yes. Is there a problem with representing my mom?" She wondered if Quinlin knew.

A dubious smile appeared on his face. "Not at all." He paused. "Mr. Turner sends you his regards."

A shiver ran down Keren's spine. She'd hoped Quinlin was out of her life forever. So much depended on getting her mom paroled, especially now that she also needed the twisted curse reversed. She had overlooked her personal feelings about Quinlin and went with the best lawyer Calypso's money could buy. Her stomach clenched. That was the same logic she used when she'd agreed Itorn could take Katrina. Hopefully, this decision wouldn't backfire on her.

He pulled out two pads of paper and two pens. "Let's get to work." He handed a pad and pen to Keren. "I've scheduled a visit with your mom tomorrow morning. I have a couple of hours to work with you on your testimony tonight."

Keren stared down at the paper. Since her mom had gone to prison, she hadn't visited her. She hadn't even contacted her until she needed her mom's help. "Does she seem," Keren paused, looking for the right word, "happy?"

Theodore frowned. "Happy doesn't describe anyone in prison."

Keren's shoulders slumped. Everything her mom had done, she'd done because she loved her daughters. Keren should have been there for her.

Theodore leaned over and put his hand over Keren's. "She's glad you reached out. She's missed you."

She swallowed the lump in her throat. "Does she know about Katrina?"

Theodore shook his head. "I haven't told her anything since I don't have all the facts. I thought it would be more like torture to dribble out guesses and half-truths." He sat up and took his pen. "High-security magic prisons restrict inmates from watching the news. Your mom doesn't know what's been going on in the world."

So much had happened since her mom went to prison. Keren had unknowingly set the dragons free, then fought to free Katrina and the Amplification Disk from the elemental realm. Then there was Azalea, a fairy, a Magic Council member, and her mom's best friend, who had sacrificed herself for Keren. Would everything overwhelm her mom? Would she want to help Keren once she knew the truth?

Keren nodded, then picked up her pen. The sooner she got this done, the sooner she could get her sister back. "Let's get to work."

CHAPTER FIVE

BRIGGS

Briggs sped down the residential street in response to a 911 call. A human family had barricaded themselves in their home during a fox-shifter attack. He ducked when the police car's rear window exploded.

"What was that!" Briggs shouted. As the rear of the car fishtailed, he steered into the movement to avoid spinning out.

A woman fox shifter landed on the car's hood. Half of her skull was raw from part of her scalp having been ripped from her head. The other half had midlength blonde air streaked with blood. She screeched at Briggs and raised her palm toward him.

Briggs opened the car door and launched himself out as a water jet exploded on the driver's seat. He hit the pavement hard, then rolled out of the way. The unmanned squad car careened into a lamppost, sending the fox shifter flying backward off the hood.

"They're getting stronger," Briggs growled to himself.

He slammed his fist into the ground. Vines pushed their way through the pavement and wrapped themselves around the female fox shifter. She screeched again while tearing at the vines. Briggs waved a hand across his body, and limbs from the trees lining the street encapsuled the fox shifter. He had the vines tie her hands behind her back and wrap around her eyes.

He gritted his teeth. These fox shifters weren't criminals. They were sick with magic frenzy. Keren had to find a cure before the world declared an all-out war against them. "That should keep you from using magic until we can sedate you."

His radio crackled, then Officer Smythe spoke. "Commander, are you alright?"

Briggs winced and grabbed his shoulder. He was getting too old for these types of maneuvers. He looked down the street and saw six police cars racing toward him.

He clicked the button on his radio. "I'm fine. Keep your guard up and your eyes open. The fox shifters are getting more aggressive."

Suddenly, as fifteen fox shifters darted from a house and toward the street, he shouted into the radio, "On your left, fifteen assailants incoming!"

The cars skidded to a halt, and two squads of inquisitors flooded onto the street, taking cover behind the cars' open doors. They split themselves into one group of eight bear shifters and one group of twelve wolf shifters. Officer Smythe stood with the wolf shifters.

The wolf-shifter inquisitors lifted their hands and sent a wave of fireballs toward the approaching fox shifters. The fireballs exploded on the ground several feet in front of the raging fox shifters.

"Stop," a voice boomed over a bullhorn. "Or next time they won't be warning shots."

Neither the threatening fireballs nor the inquisitor's verbal warning slowed the approaching fox shifters. If anything, it pushed them into a more agitated state.

A lean fox shifter wearing a business suit pushed his opened palms downward, then swooped them into the air. Briggs heard groaning, then the ground beneath him shook. Underneath the police cars, the pavement exploded. From a broken waterline, water gushed up, knocking the inquisitors off their feet. One police car flipped onto its roof.

The spouting water formed into a pillar, then split into four separate streams. Each stream curved in the air, then shot toward an inquisitor. Two bear shifters created a vine shield in time to save themselves from the full impact of the attack. The other water streams fell full force onto the other inquisitors, knocking them out of Briggs's view.

Briggs looked back at the fox shifter controlling the water streams. The fox shifter stood on the sidewalk, moving his hands through the air while the other five fox shifters launched themselves at the police cars. This one must be the leader, he thought. The inquisitors didn't stand a chance while the leader controlled the water streams.

Briggs slammed his hand into the ground. Roots and vines sprouted around the leader's feet. He jumped back before the vines took hold, and circled a hand in the air. One of the water streams turned toward the leader. It curved and ran along the ground, and when it reached the leader, it lifted him into the air. He stood atop the water stream as if it were solid ground.

"Two can play at that game," Briggs growled as he slammed his hand into the ground. Vines pushed through the ground and wrapped themselves around his waist. The vines lifted him into the air so that he hovered at eye level with the fox shifter.

Briggs waved his arm and a section of the vine segmented off. The segment reached toward the leader. From behind, a stream of water cut through the vine like a hot knife cutting through butter. Briggs shot out another vine, but the water stream cut it down again.

The inquisitors had regrouped on the ground. Half of them fought the two remaining water streams while the other half battled the fox shifters. With the water magic containing them, the inquisitors were losing ground against the fox shifters.

Briggs felt a jerk, then his vine disintegrated. While his attention had drifted to the inquisitors, the leader's water stream cut the vine suspending Briggs in the air. As he fell headfirst toward the ground, Briggs motioned for another vine. It wrapped itself around his ankle, stopping his fall just before he hit the ground.

He knew he had to take the leader out. With a sweep of his hand, the vine holding his ankle circled. Like a lasso being twirled by a cowboy, the vine whipped Briggs through the air.

Briggs clenched his fist. The timing had to be just right. The spinning was disorienting, but he focused on the leader. When he opened his fist, the vine let him go. Like a torpedo, he sailed toward the fox shifter. The leader's eyes widened, but he didn't react fast enough, and Briggs slammed into him. The impact caused the leader to lose control of his magic. The water column and streams fell to the ground, but the gushing water from the broken water pipes continued to flood the street.

Briggs wrapped his arms and legs around the fox shifter, bracing for the impact. Then the two crashed to the ground. As they rolled, Briggs kept a firm grip on the fox shifter. When they stopped rolling, Briggs pushed his hand onto the lawn. Vines sprouted up and wrapped the fox shifter within a cocoon.

Panting, Briggs rolled onto his back. One down, fourteen to go. He pushed himself onto his feet and jogged toward the police cars.

Taking out the leader had left the rest of the fox shifters disorganized and confused. Inquisitors had restrained five on the ground, while pinning nine more against a squad car. Briggs scanned the area. There were no more fox shifters in the immediate vicinity. He leaned on a police car to catch his breath as the inquisitors restrained the remaining fox shifters.

Officer Smythe walked over and put a hand on Briggs's shoulder. "Thanks for the help. Their magic is crazy."

"Anytime," Briggs said. "We need to report that the fox shifters are working together and their magic has evolved." Briggs dangled a smashed radio microphone in the air. "I damaged my radio in the fight."

"My radio has water damage." Officer Smythe nodded to the other inquisitors. "It looks like they have this under control." He tapped the roof of the police car. "We'll use the vehicle's radio." They got inside the car and contacted the station.

"This is Commander Wilson. I need to talk to the chief."

"One moment," the voice answered.

Briggs watched the inquisitors line the contained fox shifters on the ground. Those poor souls. They had no control over their illness. Then his eyes widened in horror as he watched a wolf shifter raise his palm to the first fox shifter.

"What's he doing?" Briggs asked. "Hey," he shouted out of the car's window. "What are you doing?"

The wolf shifter looked at Briggs and curled his lip. He turned his attention back to the helpless fox shifter. Then the wolf shifter's head shot back, and he fell to the ground. Two more inquisitors fell to the ground next to him.

"What's happening?" Officer Smythe asked.

"Stay here," Briggs ordered. "And stay down. We're under attack."

Briggs slipped out of the police car. In a crouched position, he moved to one of the downed inquisitors. A dart protruded from the inquisitor's chest. Briggs pressed his fingers to the inquisitor's neck. No pulse. He looked at the other downed inquisitors. Each had the same type of dart in their chest. A grunt drew Briggs's attention. Several more inquisitors fell.

"Stay down!" Briggs shouted. But the last of the inquisitors fell.

He scrambled back to the police car and got in as a dart smashed against the side window, cracking but not breaking it.

Briggs grabbed the radio. "Officers down!" he shouted. "We need ambulances and SWAT with heavy armor. The assailants have poisonous dart guns." Briggs reported their location.

"10-4," responded the voice on the radio. "Medical and SWAT are on their way to your location."

Ping. Ping. Ping. More darts struck the squad car.

"We have to get out of here." Briggs started the engine and stomped on the gas. The police car's wheels squealed as Briggs drove away from the slaughter.

"What happened back there?" Officer Smythe asked. "Who was shooting at us?"

"I don't know," Briggs growled. "But I have my suspicions." Dart rifles. A mysterious concoction that kills inquisitors. Smelled like dragons.

"Where are you going?" Officer Smythe asked. "The precinct is the other direction."

"I'm working on a hunch," Briggs said as he pushed the gas pedal to the floorboard.

As Briggs turned off Billionaires' Row, he drove down Calypso's long, curved driveway. He shook his head. Even after all the magic battles in Las Vegas, Calypso's lawn and gardens looked neat and trimmed. The dragon warlord needed to reassess his priorities.

When Briggs spotted General Zaim and a half dozen of his soldiers positioned on the lawn, his chest tightened. He glanced around, looking for Sirena. The general rarely left the Elf Princess's side.

When the police car rolled to a stop in front of Calypso's mansion, Briggs hopped out.

"Stay in the car," Briggs told Officer Smythe.

As he trotted to the door, he gave a nod to the general. The general nodded back, and Briggs felt a wave of relief. At least they were still at peace with the elves.

Briggs shook the door handle. When he found it locked, he used one hand to grab the brass ring hanging from the teeth of a dragon's head and drummed it against the door while using the fist of his other hand to bang on the door until Ryota opened it.

"I'm here to see Calypso." Briggs tried to push his way past Ryota. "Where is he?"

Ryota stood his ground, not allowing Briggs inside. "I'll announce your arrival, Commander Wilson."

Briggs stepped back. His breath came in long, heavy pants. "Yes, announce my arrival to the dragon warlord." He made sure his voice had a distinct, sarcastic tone.

Ryota tipped his head and raised an eyebrow, then stepped aside so Briggs could enter. Once Ryota shut the door, he led Briggs to the drawing room.

"Commander Wilson is here to see you, sir," Ryota said after he entered the room.

Briggs heard Calypso's exasperated voice. "My home is like a revolving door." He let out a heavy breath. "Send him in."

Ryota motioned Briggs forward. When Briggs stepped into the drawing room, he was disappointed Calypso wasn't alone.

"Gaines, Sirena," he said as he nodded to each. "Step outside. I have something to discuss with Calypso." Then his eyes locked onto the dragon warlord.

Even though Gaines and Sirena hadn't moved, Briggs couldn't wait to confront Calypso.

"I'm guessing you're responsible for this catastrophe," Briggs said, trying to control his temper.

"Catastrophes seem to be a dime a dozen these days." Calypso swirled the ice in his glass. "Which specific catastrophe are you referring to?" He gave Briggs a smug smile.

"You know very well what I'm talking about." Briggs stomped forward.

Calypso slid out from behind the bar and pulled his shoulders back. "If you're accusing me of something, Commander Wilson, come to the point. I've had a trying day."

Briggs saw Ryota step closer. He knew he didn't stand a chance against two dragons, especially when he had two innocent bystanders in the room. He took a few deep breaths to control himself.

"I am accusing you of murder." Briggs kept his eyes locked on Calypso.

Calypso raised an eyebrow. "I have," he paused, "had indiscretions in my past. However, I'm guessing that's not why you're here."

"I'm here because of your attack on two inquisitor squads." Briggs could barely get the words out. "They were rounding up fox shifters when you killed them."

"I assure you, Commander, I've been here the entire day." He drummed his fingers on the bar. "If you don't believe me, which I'm certain you don't, I have several witnesses who can attest on my behalf."

"You could have had Petrov or another dragon do your dirty work." He clenched his fists at his side. "The darts. What was in them?"

"Darts?" Gaines asked as he stepped forward. "My agents reported shifters dying from drained magic. Someone had shot them with darts."

Ignoring Gaines, Briggs continued questioning Calypso. "Why attack inquisitors, Calypso? What do you have to gain?"

Calypso relaxed and moved back behind the bar. He took a bottle off the shelf and filled his glass. "When was the last time you spoke with Keren?"

Briggs's body vibrated. "Keren has nothing to do with this." He pulled handcuffs from his belt. "I'm arresting you on suspicion of murder."

As Briggs stepped forward, Ryota blocked his path.

"Get out of the way, Ryota," Briggs said through gritted teeth. "Don't make me arrest you for impeding an officer."

"Briggs," Gaines said as he tugged on Briggs's arm, "it's not the dragons."

Briggs looked down at Gaines. "What are you talking about?"

"My PIB agents reported that shifters were killed this morning with a dart gun. I'm surprised you haven't heard about it. Hold on." He pulled out his phone. "I just received another message." He read the message and licked his lips. His eyes darted between Briggs and Calypso. "They confirmed it."

"Confirmed what?" Briggs asked.

Calypso took a sip of his drink. "Confirmed sorcerers are using Katrina's blood to eliminate shifters." He pointed at the handcuffs. "You should protect me, Commander, not arrest me."

"Briggs," Gaines put a hand on his arm, "Calypso is right. It's Itorn, not the dragons. Itorn kidnapped Katrina today."

Calypso finished his drink in one gulp and slammed the glass on the bar. "He's weaponizing her blood and plans to exterminate the shifter races."

Briggs pulled out his phone. This sounded crazy. He flipped through the multiple missed calls from Keren.

"Where's Keren?" Briggs asked. He looked up when he heard Keren's voice.

"Briggs? Where have you been?" She rushed forward. "I've been calling."

He looked guiltily at his long list of missed calls. "I see that. I'm sorry. It's a madhouse out there."

"Itorn took Katrina," she said.

Briggs wrapped his arms around her. "I just heard. I'm sorry."

"Gaines, have the agents contacted you?" Keren asked. When he didn't answer right away, she stepped away from Briggs. "Gaines? What's wrong?"

Gaines held up his phone. "The agents just confirmed the darts contained Katrina's blood. They double-checked her medical records against the samples from the darts."

"No!" Keren yelled. "I can't let him use Katrina to wipe out the shifter races!"

"You're jumping to conclusions," Briggs said. "Itorn's not my favorite person, but he's never threatened shifters."

"Because he never had a weapon." Calypso's eyes burned with rage. "The Dark Guild tried. Do you know how deep into the sorcerers' hierarchy that tainted directive went?"

"Marcus was a madman," Keren said. "He stole *The Sorcerers' Book* and turned the spells into curses."

Briggs remembered when Itorn had taken them to the elders' library. Itorn had secured the door with a powerful spell. His chest tightened. "Are you sure Marcus stole the book? Or was it given to him?"

Keren pulled back. "Mom said he stole it. She never mentioned him getting the book from anyone else. I can ask her when I see her tomorrow."

Gaines's phone buzzed. He checked the message, then pointed to the large LED screen behind the bar. "Turn on the news."

Calypso grabbed the remote and turned on the television. Everyone stood slack-jawed at the news report.

The news reporter held a hand to one ear and a microphone in the other. "I'm getting several reports." He listened for a few more seconds, then looked at the camera. "Total chaos is erupting with fox-shifter attacks. There's no logic we can detect from the attacks. They're brutal and unprovoked." He put his hand to his ear again. "Several states are declaring an emergency and calling out the National Guard." He blinked in surprise, then said in a somber tone, "Their orders are to stop the fox shifters with any force necessary. They ordered everyone to stay inside."

Calypso hit the mute button. "Humans can't decipher between shifter races. If they hate one race, they hate us all." He pointed to the screen. "This plays perfectly into Itorn's plan. No human will raise a finger to help shifters."

"I have to call the Ancients," Keren said. "Right now."

CHAPTER SIX

KEREN

"Sir, should I get the Keys to the Ancients?" Ryota asked.

A wave of Calypso's hand sent Ryota racing from the room.

Keren spun to face Gaines. "We need Nadria." She typed out a message on her phone. "Come on, Nadria," she mumbled, waiting for a reply. "Yes!" She grabbed the phone with both hands. "She's with Ordell at the Bellagio Hotel."

"I'm on it." Gaines raced from the room.

She grabbed Briggs's arm. "You'll have to stand in for the bear shifters."

Briggs's face blanched, but he nodded.

"And we need a wolf shifter," Keren said.

"Officer Smythe is outside. He's a wolf shifter. I'll bring him in." Briggs trotted out of the drawing room.

Keren remembered the last time they used the Keys to the Ancients artifact. She'd tricked the Ancients and had stolen elemental magic from them. Maybe they wouldn't show up when they summoned them. She gritted her teeth and looked at the television screen where they were showing horrific scenes of encounters with fox shifters. She had to try.

A wolf-shifter inquisitor stepped into the room. His short, stocky body had layers of muscles. His eyes flitted around the room, taking in all the details.

"Officer Smythe." Briggs clapped him on the shoulder. "This request is unorthodox, but we need your help with a magic ceremony."

He gave a terse nod. "I'll do anything to help. What do you need?"

Briggs looked at Ryota.

"You'll need to learn your part of the ritual." Ryota motioned to Briggs. "You too."

Gaines arrived with Nadria and Ordell and brought them into the drawing room. Nadria had her snow-white hair pulled back into a ponytail. Large pale-blue eyes, pulled up slightly at the edges, nervously scanned the room.

Ordell's emerald green eye locked onto Keren. Jet-black hair covered his other eye. His rail-thin body looked weak and frail. Although Ordell was a puca, the trauma from his recent kidnapping had blocked him from being able to transform into any other form.

"Keren," Nadria said. She ran over and wrapped her arms around Keren's neck. "Gaines said this was an emergency." She looked at Briggs and Officer Smythe.

Keren squeezed her friend. "I'm sorry I have to involve you in this. But I need you to help call the Ancients. I have to cure the fox shifters' magic frenzy. They're calling out the National Guard. They're going to slaughter them."

Nadria gasped and pulled away, her face pale. "Oh."

Keren squeezed Nadria's hand. "I need the Ancients to help me cure magic frenzy."

Nadria nodded but had an anxious look on her face.

"No!" Ordell shouted, pushing protectively in front of Nadria. "She's been through too much. She's not strong enough."

Nadria put her trembling hand on his shoulder. "My race needs my help. Please understand. I have to try."

Ordell looked at Nadria. "But we promised each other we'd be careful."

"I know," Nadria whispered. Her hand gently caressed Ordell's cheek. "But what other fox shifter can do this?"

Ordell wiped his face with the back of his hand, then gave her a hug and kissed her cheek. When he turned to Keren, his red-rimmed eye exposed the passionate love he felt for Nadria. "If she shows signs of weakening, you'll stop the ritual?"

With guilt clawing at her chest, Keren answered, "I will."

Keren knew Nadria was right. She was the only fox shifter in the entire world that wasn't afflicted with magic frenzy, which left her as Keren's only hope to contact the Ancients.

But Ordell was also right. Nadria hadn't fully recovered from the kidnapping. Hersal, their elf kidnapper, had not only drugged Nadria into submission but also he had plunged his hunting knife into her chest. The wound would have been mortal if Keren hadn't stolen the water-elemental magic from the Ancients to keep Nadria alive.

Ordell took a seat at the bar, his eyes never leaving Nadria.

Keren squeezed Nadria's arms. "Thank you. Ryota will teach you the words to the ceremony." She glanced over at Briggs. Something more than the ceremony was wrong. His clenched jaw and the hollow look in his eyes told her it was something serious. Afterward, she'd find out what had happened. Right now, her priority was curing magic frenzy. "Go with Briggs and Officer Smythe."

Nadria nodded and walked over to join Ryota.

Once everyone had their parts memorized, Ryota opened the small box containing the Keys to the Ancients. He pulled out a key with a bow that signified fire. He handed the fire key to Officer Smythe. The earth key went to Briggs, and the water key went to Nadria. He held the air key tight in his hand.

"Now," Ryota said. "Let's form a circle."

They moved the room's furniture to the side, then Nadria, Ryota, Briggs, and Officer Smythe moved to the center of the floor.

Briggs frowned. "Will this work?"

"We'll call them," Keren shifted uncomfortably, "but I don't know if they'll have the answers I need to cure magic frenzy."

"What if they don't? What's plan B?" Briggs asked.

The thought of not being able to cure the fox shifters sent a chill up her spine. Her shoulders deflated. They were putting all their eggs in the Ancients' basket. "Honestly, I don't know."

A long silence so heavy that Keren struggled to breathe filled the room.

Ryota cleared his throat. "Let's get to it."

The shifters extended their palms to the side, being careful not to touch their shifter neighbor or to drop their keys.

After Ryota gave him a nod, Briggs chanted, "Fertile soil nurtures."

An image of rich soil appeared in the center of the circle.

Nadria continued, "Water quenches."

A pool of water appeared in the middle of the soil.

"Fire brings new life," Officer Smythe chanted.

Flames sprouted from the pool of water.

"From the wisps of smoke, we seek the Ancients from all elements," Ryota said as he released smoke from his mouth.

The smoke swirled around the other elements, obstructing them from view, and four heads appeared in the smoke.

An Ancient spoke: "What knowledge do you seek?"

Keren stepped away from Briggs as she reached for her pulse. It shot up her neck and into the back of her eyes, causing a golden glow to dance over her skin. She called each of her elemental creatures. Four appeared behind Nadria and placed its paws on her shoulders. Two put its paws on Officer Smythe, while Three put its hands on Briggs. One did a somersault, then placed its claws on Ryota's shoulders.

"I want to cure the fox shifters' magic frenzy. How do I do that?" Keren asked.

The Ancient scowled. "The human. Again you intrude upon this sacred ritual."

Keren gritted her teeth. "I made a mistake and gave the fox shifters too much magic. How do I take it back?"

The Ancient shook his head. "You cannot."

Keren's heart raced. "I took the magic from the elemental realm. I can put it back. Tell me how."

"It's not that simple," another Ancient said. "We sacrificed ourselves to bring magic here to the elemental realm. You're human and unable to make that same sacrifice."

Keren's legs felt wobbly. "There must be a way."

"You cannot hold elemental magic." The Ancient looked at Nadria. "However, this fox shifter can."

Keren shook her head. "No."

"Keren," Nadria said in a shaky voice. "I'll do it."

"No, you won't," Ordell said as he charged at Nadria. Calypso grabbed his shoulder and pushed him back into his seat.

Nadria looked at Ordell, and tears welled in her eyes. "You know I have to," she said in a faint, quivering voice. "Who else can do this?"

Keren couldn't let Nadria sacrifice herself. All of this had happened to save Nadria's life. She wouldn't sacrifice her now. "Four," Keren blurted out. "Four can hold water elemental magic."

The Ancient frowned as all eyes turned to Four. "Your creature. Interesting."

"Keren, what are you doing?" Briggs asked.

"Fixing what I broke. No one else should have to make a sacrifice but me." She stepped forward, running her hand along Four's sleek tail. "I won't force you," she said with a shaky voice. "Would you be willing to..." her voice broke off.

"Keren," Briggs said, "what will happen to Four? What will happen to you?"

Probably the same thing that happened to the Ancients when they took elemental magic from the world. Maybe it would be different for Four. She shook her head. "I don't know."

Keren looked into Four's eyes for what seemed like an eternity. Then Four reached out its paw and placed it on Keren's head. She covered her eyes and burst into tears.

After Keren gathered herself, she looked at the Ancients. "I'll drain enough magic from the fox shifters to cure magic frenzy. Four agreed to be the vessel. But I have a conditional requirement."

"State it," the Ancient said.

Keren looked at Ordell. His lips and chin trembled as he fought against Calypso's iron grip. She looked back at the Ancients. "You give Nadria enough magic to survive the drain without giving her magic frenzy."

"We must consult on this unusual request." The Ancients huddled together. Keren heard whispers but couldn't make out what they were saying.

"We will assist with curing the fox shifters' magic frenzy. But we will not save Nadria," the Ancient said.

"Then no deal," Keren said. She clenched her fists and shouted at the Ancients, "Are you telling me you're willing to let the shifter races tear themselves apart? They are being hunted and killed as we speak. Didn't you sacrifice yourselves to avoid this exact situation?"

A woman Ancient lifted her chin. "We did not cause this situation. You did."

"I'm not denying my accountability. I did it to save Nadria. I refuse any solution that puts her at risk. I'm willing to sacrifice my beloved creature, Four." Keren fell to her knees. "Isn't that enough? I'm begging you."

Again, the Ancients took counsel with one another. When they finished, the woman spoke.

"Very well. We will do the best we can to balance Nadria's magic." She looked at Nadria. "You must stay strong. The push and pull of magic may tear you apart, regardless of our efforts."

"No!" Ordell shouted, and finally broke free.

Calypso lunged across the bar, his hand landing on Ordell's shoulder. He pulled Ordell back and pushed him down onto the barstool. "Let them proceed."

"But she's not strong enough," Ordell whimpered.

Nadria looked back at Ordell. "It's alright. I'll survive." Her comforting words didn't match her facial expression of pure terror.

Keren covered her face. She was again risking Nadria's life. One bad decision kept leading to another. One day, this insanity would stop. After a few moments, she wiped her face, then stood. "We're ready."

She put a hand on Nadria's shoulder and kissed her cheek. Then she wrapped her arms around Four's tail. "I'm sorry. Thank you."

"Four, please enter the circle," the Ancient said. "Do not break the circle during the magic transfer."

Each of the shifters nodded in agreement, and Four floated to the center of the circle. The Ancients started chanting.

A wind blew through the room, causing a vase sitting on a side table to crash to the floor.

Nadria's scream echoed over the blustering wind. Her legs almost buckled, endangering the connection to the Ancients, but Keren caught Nadria and grabbed her wrists. Keren forced Nadria to keep her arms extended.

More unintelligible chanting came from the Ancients. Then wisps of black, gold, and white pulled from Nadria's chest and floated to Four. Four stood statue-still as the wisps entered its body.

As Keren felt Nadria's body convulse, she wondered if she should stop the ceremony. If she let Nadria's arms fall, this nightmare would end. But breaking the circle might hurt Nadria or the others. No, this had to happen. Keren gritted her teeth and held Nadria in place.

Another scream from Nadria had Ordell clawing at Calypso's arm.

"Ordell, stay put. If you break the circle, Nadria will die!" Calypso yelled.

Smaller wisps circled Nadria's feet. They ran up her legs and entered her through her stomach. Her body jerked and convulsed again, but Keren kept her upright and in the circle. Then Nadria went limp in Keren's arms.

A sudden flash of light temporarily blinded Keren. The wind died down, and she blinked away the dots to see what was going on.

Four had vanished, and the Ancients were floating in the center of the circle.

"It is done," an Ancient said. Then they all disappeared.

Keren collapsed backward onto the floor with Nadria's limp body falling on top of her.

"Nadria!" Ordell shouted.

Keren saw Ordell's haggard face. A look of horror was etched on every inch. Please, she thought. Please let Nadria be alive.

CHAPTER SEVEN

QUINLIN

Quinlin walked the perimeter of his limited exercise yard. The concrete walls stood eleven feet high with barbed wire on the top. Four rifle barrels trained directly on him jutted out from window slits on the wall across from the prison door. A cloudy sky loomed over the metal grate secured across the top. The light drizzle felt cool on his exposed face and hands.

Too-tight handcuffs bit into his wrists, securing his hands behind his back, while chains around his ankles limited him to half steps, forcing him to walk like a ninety-year-old man. As he pulled each foot free of the inch-thick mud covering the ground, they made sickly suction sounds.

Isolation rules required him to keep moving for the entire hour. He didn't mind since this was the only time he escaped the guards' abuse. Quinlin could take the guards jeering at him and insulting him with every perverse name imaginable. What he couldn't stand was the physical abuse. A slimy-haired weasel of a guard had dubbed him "pretty boy" when he arrived, and things had gone downhill from there. His bruised ribs made every breath sharp, but he couldn't let the pain show on his face. That would only make the beatings more severe. He questioned how long he'd survive.

From the knees down, his pants were wet and mud splattered. He'd already taken his one rationed shower today, so he'd be sleeping in these soggy clothes. When he heard the click of the internal door lock, he didn't react.

"Pretty boy," a gruff voice shouted as the sound of at least six firearms cocked in preparation.

Quinlin stopped moving. He flexed his fingers, trying to increase the blood circulation. Magic dampening only worked inside the prison. Out here in the yard, if he were free from these handcuffs, he could cast a spell. The yard was the prison's weakness. In time, he'd learn how to exploit it.

"Get over here. It's time to get back to your hole," the guard said.

Quinlin turned and trudged toward the short, pudgy guard standing in the doorway. When Quinlin came within arm's reach, the guard drove his fist into Quinlin's stomach. With his ribs screaming in pain, Quinlin doubled over. He could headbutt this chunky guard and knock him off his feet, but the others would tear him apart. It was better to let the guard believe he had the upper hand.

The guard grabbed Quinlin's arm and tugged him inside. "Get moving, pretty boy."

Quinlin stumbled when another guard kicked him in the butt. The chain between his ankles was too short for him to stop the fall. He twisted to one side and landed on his back. On impulse, he drew his knees up. Both feet shot out, kicking the closest guard's kneecap backward. The guard's wailing followed the sickening crack. Too bad it hadn't been the chunky guard. That might've been worth what Quinlin knew was to come.

In seconds, steel-toed boots bludgeoned him from all directions. Quinlin curled into a fetal position to protect himself the best he could, but nothing could block the brutal attack.

When the kicking stopped, the guards hauled Quinlin up by his arms and dragged him to his cell. They tossed him in and locked the door, without unshackling his restraints.

"You need to learn some manners, pretty boy," the chunky guard said. "I hear the woman who testified against you is getting a parole hearing." The guard laughed. "That's right, pretty boy. While you're here rotting in jail for the rest of your life, she's going scot-free."

Quinlin lay motionless on the floor. He had quickly learned the guards preferred moving targets, so he frequently pretended to be subdued to avoid extended beatings. But this time, he didn't have to pretend. He had to get out of this torture chamber.

When Keren had approached his law firm to represent her mother, Quinlin couldn't believe his luck. Keren could be the key to escaping this hell.

After hearing the guards' retreating footsteps, Quinlin let out a groan. He pushed himself to his knees with his elbows. Blood dribbled from his face and puddled on the floor.

The only consolation for his miserable state had been knowing Keren's mom faced the same life as he did. But he'd gladly set her free himself if it also meant his freedom. His plan depended on the decision of the parole board.

Keren's face flashed in his mind. She'd been so beautiful and so cunning when she'd outsmarted him at Church Street Station. He should be angry with her, but oddly, he felt proud. Few people were clever enough to get the better of him.

CHAPTER EIGHT

KEREN

Keren struggled to breathe while Nadria's weight crushed her chest. She felt as though the Ancients had torn her body to pieces.

"Nadria!" Ordell yelled. "Oh my gosh, please be OK!"

After the weight lifted, Keren took a deep breath. Strong arms slipped under her knees and shoulders. The smell of the forest after a rain shower told her Briggs had picked her up. She heard his heart pounding in his chest.

"Keren," he whispered, "are you alright?"

She tried to force herself to talk, but she couldn't. Her eyes felt glued shut. I'm not, she silently screamed.

"She's unconscious, but I feel a pulse," Briggs said.

She felt movement. Then Briggs laid her down on something soft. He grabbed her hand.

"Keren." She felt a tap on her cheek. "Wake up."

With effort, she forced her eyes open.

"Oh, thank goodness." Briggs kissed her hand. She felt a blanket tuck up and around her. The soft cotton felt good against her clammy skin.

She turned her head to look at Briggs. Worried lavender eyes stared back at her.

"Nadria?" Keren's throat burned with the effort. "Alive?"

"Yes, she's alive, and she shows no signs of magic frenzy. Smythe and Ryota are looking after her." He squeezed her hand. "I'm going to call the station to find out if the ceremony cured the fox shifters we have in custody. I'll be right back."

As the warmth of his hand left her, a chill ran through her body. Briggs stepped away and pulled out his phone.

"This is Commander Wilson. I need to speak with the chief immediately." He paused a moment. "Chief, the ceremony to drain the fox shifters' magic is complete." Again, he went silent. Briggs paced the floor. "Yes, I'm here. Uh-huh. I see. Alright, I'll check in later." He hung up and rushed back to Keren.

"The chief has called a cease-fire on the fox shifters until they can confirm the ceremony cured magic frenzy." He took her hand. "Can I get you anything?"

A tear dripped from Keren's eye. She needed Four. The painful void inside her felt larger than a moon crater.

She took a ragged breath. "Hold me."

Briggs wrapped his arms around her and leaned in close. "You'll be alright." He gave her a squeeze. "That was unbelievable."

Another tear dripped from her eye. Four had sacrificed itself to fix her mistake—or at least she hoped the sacrifice had fixed her mistake.

Briggs's phone buzzed. "Sorry, I'll be right back." He stood and walked to the other side of the room. "Commander Wilson."

Keren watched as he scrubbed a hand through his red hair.

"I see. What about Jordon?" Briggs let out a sigh while tipping his head back. "That's good news. Thank you for getting back to me so quickly."

Briggs turned to her and smiled. "Officers are reporting fox shifters dazed and confused but with no signs of magic frenzy. They're doing a sweep of the city to see if anyone needs medical help." He walked to the couch and squatted down so his face was level with Keren's. "And the best news is that Jordon's eyes are back to normal. They've stopped the sedation treatment for him and all other fox shifters in custody."

Keren gave him a weak smile. "That is good news." She shifted, trying to push herself up.

"Whoa," Briggs said as he put a hand on her shoulder. "Where do you think you're going?"

"Help me sit up," Keren said. She felt relieved magic frenzy was under control, but Katrina was still Itorn's prisoner.

"Are you sure?" Briggs put his hands under her arms and lifted her to a sitting position. "I think you should stay on the couch. You've been through a lot." He tucked the blanket around her legs.

"There's no time." Keren scrubbed both hands through her hair. She blinked her eyes to focus. "Remember when Itorn took us to the elders' library? He told us a strong protection spell safeguarded the library. It's hard to believe Marcus had somehow broken into the elder's library to steal *The Sorcerers' Book*." She put her hand on Briggs's arm. "I think you were onto something. Either Marcus was stronger than an elder sorcerer and broke into the library, then sealed it back up to cover his tracks, or someone helped him."

"It looks that way," Briggs said.

Keren shook her head. "If an elder sorcerer and Marcus conspired to steal the book, the danger is greater than I'd realized." She grabbed Briggs's arm. "I have to protect Katrina. Her antimagic would interest several potentially dangerous groups."

"I agree. Once the high alert is over for fox shifters, I'll ask the chief to help search for Katrina," Briggs said. "And I'll talk to Gaines to see if his agents have any information on Itorn's location."

"Thanks." Keren ran a hand over Briggs's cheek. "There's something else I need you to do for me."

He smiled. "What do you need?" He tucked the blanket tighter around her legs.

"I need the evidence that was taken from my house when they arrested Mom."

Briggs looked shocked. "What? Why?"

"I want Mom to reverse the twisted curse. That way, Katrina will lose her antimagic, or whatever that negative force is, and no one will want to use her. Not ever again."

"But you'll lose your magic too," Briggs said. "Have you thought this through?"

"Yes." All this was her fault. She hung her head. "I was never meant to have elemental magic."

She could no longer hold in the emotion. Keren covered her face with her hands as a flood of tears streamed down her face. Her shoulders shook as she sobbed. She drew her knees to her chest.

Briggs sat on the couch and wrapped his arms around her. He simply held and rocked her, allowing her the release.

When she finally stopped crying, she used her shirt to wipe her face. "Briggs, I need you to do this for me." She looked him in the eye and took his hand. "It's the only way."

"What if reversing the curse hurts you or Katrina? Or worse, what if it kills you? Does your mom even know if she can reverse the curse?"

"That's why she'll need her notes." She squeezed his hand. "It's the safest way. Without her notes, she'll have to go by memory."

Briggs rested his forehead on hers. "I don't know, Keren. I have no reason to check out that evidence. It'll be hard to justify."

"I know I'm asking a lot," Keren said. "But I have to get it."

Briggs sighed. "So, what I'm hearing is you'll try to get the evidence if I don't help you."

Keren remembered what Itorn had said about her putting Briggs's career in jeopardy. Still, she couldn't lie to Briggs. He'd have to make up his own mind. "It's our best hope for saving Katrina."

"Don't you need Katrina here to undo the curse?" Briggs asked. "What if we can't find her?"

Keren shivered. The thought of not finding Katrina made her sick.

"I'm sorry," Briggs said. "But you know that's a possibility."

"I'm not sure. But I think Mom will have a better chance of reversing the curse if she has her notes."

"And what if your mom doesn't get her parole?" Briggs always played devil's advocate. Keren knew it would take serious finagling on Briggs's part to convince the Orlando chief inquisitor to release such dangerous evidence.

Keren leaned back. "Then we'll find another sorcerer to reverse the curse." She put her hands on the sides of his face. "This is the only way." She sighed and pressed her forehead to his. "I have to fix this. I'm tired of causing catastrophes."

"No," he whispered. "You stopped the Dark Guild."

"But that set off a cascade of problems. This power isn't natural. It's too easy to tip the magic scale."

After a long silence, Briggs spoke. "I'll see what I can do." He kissed the top of her head. "I'm going to call the station for an update on Jordon." He smiled at her. "You'll be alright here?"

Keren nodded. "Yeah, I'm fine." She grabbed his hand. "Thank you. I love you."

He gave her a warm smile. "I love you too."

Ordell took Briggs's place on the couch. "We think Nadria's going to be OK. She's resting in a bedroom." He hung his head. "I'm sorry about Four. That was very brave of you both." He scooted closer and put his arm around Keren, pulling her close. "She's worried about you. How are you doing?"

"I'm scared," Keren whispered.

Ordell rubbed Keren's arm. "I know. We all are. But you, Nadria, and I are together. And Briggs is here. All your friends are here to support you."

"What if it didn't work for all the fox shifters? And Four's sacrifice was for nothing?"

Before Ordell could answer, Sirena walked into the drawing room and made a beeline for the couch.

"Can I join you?" she asked, then sat on the floor by Keren's feet. "So it's true. Four's gone?" Sirena asked.

Keren nodded. "Yes."

"It's a shame," she said. "Four was so beautiful."

Keren's stomach clenched. She didn't need to be reminded of that.

"Sirena," Ordell said, "let's not talk about that right now. Keren's upset."

"Oh, sorry. I didn't mean to. I mean I only ..."

"It's alright," Ordell said in a soothing voice as he stroked Keren's hair. "Let's just sit with her. Right now, she needs our support."

"Right." Sirena wiggled closer to Keren. "What do you want to talk about?"

CHAPTER NINE

BRIGGS

After Briggs left Keren, he waved for Officer Smythe to join him. "Let's get back to the station."

They ran into Gaines on their way out.

"How'd it go?" Gaines asked. "Things seemed pretty intense."

"So far, it looks like the ceremony cured the fox shifters' magic frenzy," Briggs said.

Gaines let out a heavy breath as he ran his hand over his head. "That's such good news." He motioned to the drawing room. "Is everyone alright?"

Briggs's chest clenched. Nothing about this was alright. Keren had sacrificed one of her creatures and had put both herself and Nadria at risk. "Everyone survived, except for Four, Keren's water-elemental creature. It took the extracted water magic back to the elemental realm."

"It's not coming back?" Gaines asked.

"I don't know. Right now, it's gone." Briggs put a hand on Gaines's shoulder. "We appreciate that the PIB is working to find Katrina. Have the agents made any headway?"

"Actually, they have a couple of leads. They're following up on them now. With the number of dart attacks on shifters in Las Vegas, we believe Itorn stayed local." Gaines patted Briggs's arm. "The PIB will find Itorn." He smiled. "It's only a matter of time."

Time. That was a precious commodity. Briggs nodded to Gaines and led Officer Smythe outside. If the twisted curse were reversed, and Katrina lost her antimagic, what would Itorn do to Katrina? Would he take his anger out on Katrina to get back at Keren? Gaines needed to find Itorn and Katrina soon.

Officer Smythe and Briggs got into the police car and pulled away from Calypso's mansion. From the driver's seat, Briggs glanced at Officer Smythe. The officer sat expressionless and stared out the front window. The ceremony was way outside what a shifter would normally experience.

"You've been quiet since we left. What's on your mind?" Briggs asked. Maybe he should swing by the hospital and have Smythe treated for shock.

"That was insane," Officer Smythe said. He turned to look at Briggs. "You seem unfazed." Pausing, he cupped his hand over his mouth. He shook his head and pointed at Briggs. "She's your girlfriend. Are you just used to such intense experiences?" His hand pressed against his chest. "I'm not. I never want to do anything like that again."

"With Keren, I've learned to roll with whatever happens." Briggs thought back to the time before Keren discovered her magic. Those were simple days when the most stress he had was deciding whether to tell Keren how he felt about her. Maybe reversing the twisted curse was the best thing for everyone.

Officer Smythe shook his head. "You're a better shifter than I. I couldn't do it. I just want things to go back to normal."

Normal. Briggs laughed to himself. What did normal even look like? After they pulled up to the station, Briggs turned to Smythe.

"Thanks again for helping. You go inside. I'll be just a minute."

"Do you think it really worked?" Officer Smythe asked.

"I hope so," Briggs said.

After Smythe went into the station, Briggs pulled out his phone and dialed a familiar number. "Hi, Mabel. This is Commander Wilson."

The croaky voice of the Orlando inquisitors' station's receptionist spoke a bit too loudly. "Commander Wilson, it's nice to hear your voice. How can I help you?"

He sighed. "I need to speak to the chief."

"You're in luck. He just returned from a meeting with the mayor." She let out two raspy coughs before continuing. "Can you believe what's going on with magic frenzy? The chief insists that I have an officer escort me to and from the office."

Briggs winced as he thought of the upheaval and fear everyone had been living under. "That's a good call, Mabel. You can't be too careful. Can you put me through to the chief?"

"Of course. One minute. It was nice talking to you," Mabel said.

He tried to take the worry out of his voice. "Yes, nice talking to you too."

That brief conversation stirred homesickness in him. As long as Keren was in Las Vegas, he'd stay here. But he missed his friends and his old neighborhood. The chief's voice interrupted his thoughts.

"Briggs," the chief said. "When are you coming back to Orlando? We're in the middle of this magic frenzy crisis, and I could use you here."

"Sir," Briggs said, "we believe Keren cured magic frenzy."

"Cured? This is the first I've heard. Let me contact the mayor. If Keren actually cured this blasted illness, I'll get the papers to print an article with you, me, and Keren in the headline."

Briggs remembered the chief's obsession with his reelection. "That's unnecessary, sir." Briggs felt his collar tightening around his neck. He hated being the center of attention.

"Nonsense. When an officer of mine saves the world, the world should know."

Briggs sighed, knowing talking the chief out of any positive publicity was a losing battle. "Sir, I need a favor."

"What is it, Commander?"

Briggs bit his lip. He had to make the lie sound legitimate. "I'm investigating the origin of magic frenzy. And I believe it's the Dark Guild."

"The Dark Guild!" the chief shouted. "What makes you believe they're involved?"

"Right now, it's only a suspicion." Briggs took a deep breath. "But to be sure, we need the evidence taken at the time of Olivia Stewart's arrest."

Silence filled the air and a bead of sweat dripped down Briggs's face.

The chief's voice changed to a stoic tone. "I need more information before I can release those records. You know how dangerous those documents would be in the wrong hands."

"Yes, sir, I do. I wouldn't ask if it wasn't important." Briggs cleared his throat. "An elder sorcerer here has gone missing. We believe he's targeting shifters. Somewhere in those records might be the key."

"What makes you believe he's associated with the Dark Guild?" the chief asked.

"Two dead squads of inquisitors in Las Vegas." Briggs felt his body tense as he pictured the scene of the inquisitors dropping in the street. "We have evidence that points to the elder sorcerer being the perpetrator."

"Two squads!" the chief shouted. "What's your evidence?"

Sweat broke out on Briggs's forehead. He'd never lied to the chief before. But he couldn't disclose information about Katrina. "He has created a tainted potion that drains shifter magic. He uses dart guns to inject the potion. We've traced the dart guns used back to him."

"Good work, Commander. If that evidence will stop the inquisitor killer, I'll send it to you by special courier."

Briggs breathed a sigh of relief as he gave the chief Calypso's address. "I appreciate this."

"Just catch those murderous sorcerers. And, Briggs?"

"Yes, Chief?"

"I'm part of this investigation. Keep me informed of any breakthroughs."

To splash all over the news, thought Briggs. "Yes, sir. No problem."

"Alright then. I'm shipping the evidence overnight. You'll have it first thing in the morning."

"Thank you, sir." Briggs breathed a sigh of relief as he hung up.

CHAPTER TEN

KEREN

The next morning, Theodore arrived at 9 a.m. to pick Keren up for their forty-five-minute drive to the prison. Every muscle in her body ached as if she had worked out the entire day yesterday.

She fought back tears as she thought of Four. I will not cry, she told herself. This is almost over. I have to be strong. As Theodore drove down the road, Keren's stomach rumbled.

"Do you want to get breakfast?" Theodore looked at his watch. "We have time."

"No, thanks," Keren said.

"Are you ready to see your mom?" Theodore asked.

Keren stared straight ahead, looking at the trees that lined the two-lane highway. This time of year, their branches were thick with leaves. Some trees stood separate, looking as though they were part of a horror-movie set with moss dripping from their brown, bare branches. That's how she felt: like a tree isolated and fighting to not be overwhelmed.

"I'm ready," she said. She clasped her hands in her lap, wishing she were anywhere but here.

"The mayor of Las Vegas herself gave approval for your mom to live in the city," Theodore said. When Keren didn't respond, he continued. "Do you know the mayor?"

"I've never met her," Keren said. She knew the mayor wanted her city back to normal, which meant getting the dragons, and now the elves, out of Las Vegas. Since Keren seemed to be the link connecting everything together, the mayor must have thought it in her best interest to move things along as quickly as possible. "Calypso probably knows her."

"Calypso," Theodore repeated. "He has deep pockets."

Theodore was fishing for more information, but Keren thought the less he knew, the better.

"All casino owners have money," she said, then changed the topic. "How long until we get there?"

"Just another ten minutes," Theodore said. He took the hint and stopped asking questions. They rode in silence the rest of the way to the prison.

Indian Springs, Nevada, was home to two high-security prisons. One, nicknamed "Supermax," held the most notorious human criminals. The other, nicknamed "the Dungeon," held magic-race criminals.

As Theodore pulled off the main road and followed signs to the Dungeon, Keren admired the Rocky Mountain backdrop.

"Don't let the scenery fool you. This is a harsh area. These two prisons are called 'control units,' which is a step above maximum security. They confine prisoners twenty-three hours a day in single-occupancy cells." He turned down another road, and the prison came into view. "They poured the cell walls in the Dungeon using reenforced concrete made with an ancient elf artifact and mixed with fairy magic to impede the use of magic. They have a high ratio of staff to inmates."

Once inside, it took almost an hour to get through all the paperwork and security scans. A prison guard led Keren and Theodore to an interrogation room. Before the prison guard opened the door, she gave them instructions.

"There's a two-way mirror. We're not recording your communications with the prisoner because of lawyer-client privileges." The guard studied Keren's face. "You look like her." Then she frowned. "There's no physical contact allowed. Anything, even brushing hands, will end the visit immediately." She raised her eyebrows. "Do you understand?"

Keren felt Theodore's hand on her shoulder. "We do. We appreciate the private visit. We'll call if we need you," he said.

The guard shrugged. "You seem to have influence in high places." She squinted. "That doesn't mean you can bend the rules."

"Understood," Theodore said. "Is my client inside?"

"Yes. I'll be out here. You have a half hour. If you want to leave early, knock on the door."

"Thank you." Theodore turned the handle and opened the door. Keren followed him inside.

It felt as though the temperature of the room had dropped ten degrees. The smell of stale cigarette smoke blasted Keren in the face as she stepped inside.

Then she saw her mom sitting on one side of a rectangular metal table. Two cheap plastic chairs were sitting on the other side of the table. Thick handcuffs secured her mom's hands behind her back. Her long dark hair, now streaked with gray, rested in a low ponytail at the base of her neck. She'd been in prison for less than six months, but she looked a decade older.

When her mom turned her head, her eyes met Keren's. The sadness radiating from those hollow eyes threatened to rip Keren's heart from her chest.

Her mom didn't smile. She simply stared at Keren.

Keren forced herself to hold eye contact with her mom as she lowered herself into one of the plastic chairs. Theodore sat in the chair next to Keren and placed his briefcase on the table.

"I'm glad you came," Keren's mom said to her. When she glanced at Keren's elf ears, she frowned. A look of confusion passed over her face.

Keren hoped she wouldn't ask about her ears. Explaining about Sirena would take far longer than the half-hour visitation limit.

Her mom's eyes flicked to Theodore, then back to Keren. "I still don't understand why you hired a new lawyer. What happened to Shawn?"

"He's been sick," Keren said as she fidgeted in her chair, now self-conscious about her appearance. As she ran her hands through her hair, she brushed against her elf ears. Even though she knew it wouldn't totally conceal her ears, she pulled her hair around them.

Up close, her mom looked even older. Fine lines that had appeared on the outsides of her eyes a year ago had changed to deeper creases. Worry lines had sprouted between her eyebrows. Prison life had taken its toll.

"I'm sorry I didn't come sooner," Keren said. "It's just," she looked down at her hands, "I had to sort out my thoughts." The air thickened in the room. After completely ignoring her mom, now Keren was here to ask for her help.

"It was worth the wait," her mom said. "Can you forgive me?"

Keren lifted her head. Tears shimmered in her mom's eyes. After everything Keren had been through, she understood how hard it was to make difficult decisions to save someone you loved and to do whatever it took to save their lives. Still, she couldn't get it out of her mind that none of this would have happened if her mom hadn't joined the Dark Guild to begin with. Sitting there, staring into her mom's face, she wondered if she could ever truly forgive her.

Keren took a deep breath. "Yes," she said.

For the first time since Keren walked into the room, her mom smiled. But her eyes showed she doubted Keren's words. Her mom knew her so well.

"I'm so relieved," her mom said.

Theodore opened his briefcase and set a paper down in front of Keren's mom. "We have an emergency parole hearing this afternoon. If everything goes well, you should be home tomorrow." He set another copy of the paper in front of Keren. "Since Keren has moved to Las Vegas, we're asking for special permission for your parole to be managed from there." He pointed to a section on the page in front of Keren's mom. "I have a deposition from the mayor approving your residency in Las Vegas. It might seem like overkill, but I want as many chips on our side of the table as possible."

Keren shifted in her seat as she read along on her paper. It listed her address as Calypso's mansion. The only reason Keren had agreed to the arrangement was because she had been living in the vacant Las Vegas resorts. In order for her mom to be released, she needed a permanent address.

"Las Vegas?" her mom asked. "What made you want to move there? What about your friends?"

Without looking up from the page, Keren answered, "They're there too." Awkward silence filled the room. She might as well get straight to the point.

Keren looked up, meeting her mom's gaze. "I have two urgent requests."

Her mom frowned. "What requests?"

Keren tried to unscramble the feelings she had for her mom, but she only found disappointment and sadness. Still, her mom's expertise was Keren's best hope. "I need your help to reverse a curse on a Chinese dragon."

Her mom's eyes widened. "A Chinese dragon?"

Keren nodded. "Yes, a sorcerer cast the curse. I need you to reverse it."

"I-I ..." her mom stammered. "I can't promise anything."

Keren frowned. This had been a mistake. She'd known it was a long shot.

"But I'll try." Her mom spoke in a desperate tone as she leaned forward. "I can research." She looked from Keren to Theodore. "I'll do everything in my power. Just, please, get me out of here."

"A condition for your parole will be a strict no-magic agreement," Theodore said. "There's no way we'll get around that."

Keren's mom was visibly shaking, her calm demeanor smashed by the thought of having to serve out her five-year sentence.

"I'll agree to anything." She looked at Keren. "I'll do anything. Just, please, get me out."

When Keren saw the wild look in her mom's eyes, she felt a sharp pain in her chest. What had they done to her? Then she sighed and did her best to keep her emotions in check. "You haven't heard the second request."

"What is it?" her mom asked in a tentative voice.

"I want you to reverse the twisted curse you cast on me and Katrina."

Her mom sucked in a breath. "That was so long ago." Her eyes wandered. "It was something I cast on impulse to save you."

"Do you think it can be reversed?" Keren asked.

Her mom frowned. "I think any curse can be reversed, given enough time to research." She looked up at Keren. "I'd need my notes. After I cast the curse, I wrote everything I could remember in my journal. I also marked the page in Marcus's grimoire so I wouldn't forget which version of his curse he used." She shook her head. "But the inquisitors confiscated everything from the house when they arrested me."

"If you had your notes, could you do it? Reverse the twisted curse?" Keren leaned on the table. "Lives depend on it."

Her mom visibly swallowed, then sat back in her chair. "I understand. I think I can do it." A worried look passed over her face. "These reversals will take a strong sorcerer, maybe two." She glanced at Theodore, then back at Keren. "If I can't use my magic, are you strong enough?"

A knock sounded on the door, then the guard cracked it open. "Your time is up."

Theodore put the papers back in his briefcase and stood up. "We'll see you at the hearing." He looked at Olivia. "We can't mention anything about our discussion here. Do you understand?"

Her mom nodded. "I do." She looked at Keren. "I love you."

Keren's heart melted. She understood why her mom had cast the twisted curse: she'd done it to protect her children. But Keren knew her own sorcerer magic wasn't strong enough to reverse the curses. A wave of guilt ran over her. She planned to use her mom's research skills, then ask her to violate her parole and perform magic. Most likely, they'd send her mom back to prison with no option for another parole.

"I love you too. See you soon," Keren said. Then she followed Theodore out of the room. He flashed Keren a look once they were in the hall. "Let's catch a quick lunch before the hearing."

Theodore took Keren to a classic diner, complete with chrome metal and retro red-vinyl barstools. They'd purposefully settled themselves into a corner booth away from the other patrons.

While Theodore chomped his way through his burger like a competitive speed eater, Keren poked at the burger and fries on her plate. Normally, nothing kept her from eating. But her plan to have her mom reverse the curses had her stomach tied in knots.

Theodore used his napkin to wipe some ketchup from the corner of his mouth. He frowned at her. "You've eaten nothing all day. Are you feeling alright?"

She picked up a french fry and eyed it as if she'd never seen one before. Theodore couldn't know about her hesitation regarding her mom. "I'm fine, just worried about the parole hearing."

"You shouldn't worry. Your testimony is solid. And it's not a courtroom like you see on television shows. Seven members of the parole board will attend." He pushed his empty plate to the side and opened his briefcase sitting next to him. After searching for a few seconds, he pulled out a paper. "There will be two psychiatrists, one retired judge, one pastor, two social workers, and one ex-convict."

Keren nodded and set the french fry on her plate. "I'm not concerned with speaking in front of people." Her emotions teetered as she wondered what a worse outcome would be: her mom not getting paroled and Keren having to find another way to reverse the curses, or her mom getting paroled and Keren being responsible if her mom was sent back to prison after breaking her parole. She felt guilty about asking her mom to take that risk.

Theodore leaned his arms on the table. "Then what?"

Keren shrugged. Not wanting to let Theodore know what she was really thinking, she made up an excuse. "What if they ask something we didn't prepare for?"

He leaned back and smiled. After closing his briefcase, Theodore put a twenty-dollar bill on the table. "Highly unlikely. But if it happens, answer honestly. That's your best strategy. Most people can see through lies."

She nodded. "OK." Theodore hadn't seen through her lies and doubts during their testimony practice, but the parole board might. Her lying skills had always been subpar. She shook her head and pushed away the doubts. This was her best chance to save Jewel and Katrina. This was best for everyone.

"What if your mom doesn't make parole?" Theodore asked. "You said you'd find another way. What's your plan?"

Keren sighed. "I haven't thought about that." She tore small pieces off her napkin and tossed them on the table. "I'd ask Gaines if he knows any reliable sorcerers. Maybe they'd help."

Theodore lowered his voice. "What if I told you I know a powerful sorcerer waiting to help you?"

Keren froze midtear. Something in Theodore's eyes made her skin crawl. "You?" she asked.

He chuckled. "I'm a low-grade sorcerer. My talents are in the courtroom. I'm speaking of someone else."

Keren frowned. "Who?"

An evil smile spread across Theodore's face. "I've arranged a visit for you with Mr. Turner."

Keren's head spun. The room faded, and she thought she might pass out. Why would she visit Quinlin? She gripped the table to steady herself. "I'm not visiting Quinlin," she said in a stern voice.

Theodore held up his hands. "Here me out."

"No," Keren interrupted. "I want nothing to do with that man."

Theodore sat back. "Quinlin knows his father's curses by heart. He knows how your mom's twisted curse morphed those curses to create you. I'm certain he'd also be able to decipher the curse on Jewel."

Keren shook her head, wishing Theodore would stop talking. But a voice inside of her told her to listen. "Quinlin can't help me from jail."

"Exactly." Theodore looked around to see if anyone was listening. Then he leaned forward and said in a soft tone, "That's why you're going to break him out."

"Break him out?" Keren hissed. "Are you crazy?"

A smile crept across Theodore's face. "On the contrary. Quinlin has a plan."

"Mom will help me. We already have a plan to get Mom out of prison." Keren felt her heart pounding in her chest. She didn't like the look on the lawyer's face. "Don't we?"

Theodore scooped up the papers and put them back in his briefcase. "I've done the best I can to secure and prepare for your mother's parole hearing." He closed the briefcase, then looked at Keren. "Be realistic, Keren. Open your eyes and look at what's going on in the world right now. People are running in fear of any race with magic. Do you really think a parole board will release anyone with an ounce of magic ability?"

Keren's mouth went dry. She clasped her hands in her lap to stop them from shaking. "I'm not giving up. I'm certain they'll grant her parole."

While checking his watch, Theodore slid out of the booth. "We'll see. Come on, it's time to go back."

Dazed, Keren followed him out of the diner. Going to the law firm that was representing Quinlin had been a mistake. She felt heat rising on her neck. She wasn't some simpleton who Theodore could manipulate. Once outside, she grabbed his shoulder and turned him to face her.

"Did you sabotage my mom's hearing?" Keren demanded.

"No," he said. "I filed every motion I could to get your mom released."

Keren narrowed her eyes. "I'm not sure I believe you."

"Have Shawn double-check my work. You'll find everything is legitimate." He tipped his head. "I wouldn't do anything to jeopardize my firm." He opened the passenger-side door. "Shall we?"

Keren slid into the seat. They drove back to the prison in silence. Her stomach churned as she thought about the hearing. If it didn't go well and they kept her mom in custody, would Keren be willing to do something as extreme as breaking Quinlin out of jail? The idea gnawed at the back of her mind.

Keren rubbed her temples as Theodore filled out the required paperwork at the prison desk. Everything was unraveling. Doubts about the parole hearing flooded her mind. Her home and job were fictitious, something created on the fly by Calypso. He'd even backdated pay stubs to make it look like she'd been his employee for several months. That was a federal crime. If she went through with her testimony, she'd be as guilty as Calypso. And now she knew Theodore had the ulterior motive of breaking Quinlin out of jail.

The heavy door to the prison buzzed, and a guard opened it from the other side.

"This way," the guard said.

Theodore motioned for Keren to walk through first. The guard wore a standard blue shirt with black pants. Her belt held a gun, a Taser, handcuffs, and something else Keren couldn't make out. The rubber soles of her highly polished shoes made faint squeaking sounds as she led them down the hall.

The guard stopped outside a room with double doors. "This is your hearing room." She motioned to the door. "The parole board is already inside. Once you're settled, I'll bring in Ms. Stewart."

With a deep breath, Keren reached for the handle and opened the door. The room had a gray tiled floor, like her high school cafeteria. Barred windows lined one wall, allowing the sun to streak the tiled floor and emphasize the fact they were in a prison. At the far side were two rectangular tables. Seven people sat at the tables, reading through papers and talking to one another. One man sat to the side at a wooden desk with a steno machine.

An older gentleman with salt-and-pepper hair looked up. He gave her and Theodore a wide, toothy grin.

"You must be Ms. Stewart and Mr. Hopkins," he said. "I'm Pastor Declan. Please come in and have a seat."

When Keren didn't move, Theodore took her elbow and directed her to the half dozen black folding chairs positioned in front of the table.

"I'm sorry for the accommodations," the pastor said as he stood. "This was the best we could do on such short notice."

"Nice to meet you. We appreciate your efforts," Theodore said as he sat in one chair and scooted another in front of him as a makeshift table. He put his briefcase on the chair and opened it. "Do you have the petition?"

Pastor Declan looked down at the table, then back up at Theodore. "We do." He looked at Keren standing next to Theodore. "Do you need anything, Ms. Stewart?"

Keren realized the others had looked up from their paperwork, and all eyes were staring at her. "No. Please call me Keren." She quickly lowered herself onto the seat next to Theodore. The cold, hard metal made it difficult to get comfortable. She pushed her hands between her legs to warm them.

When the door opened behind her, Keren turned. The same guard that had escorted them to the room stepped aside to let Keren's mom enter.

Keren gaped when she saw her mom. She looked nothing like she had this morning. The frightened, cowering person had turned into a confident businesswoman. She wore a dark blue suit with a white blouse and had her hair tied into a neat bun. Keren's mom had used her expert makeup skills to hide her sunken cheeks under a brushing of blush, and she had made her lips look fuller with a shiny, pink lipstick.

"Ms. Olivia Stewart," the guard said.

Paster Declan nodded. "Bring her in. She can have a seat over there." He motioned to an area away from Keren and Theodore.

The guard walked over and moved one of the folding chairs to where the pastor had pointed. Keren's mom took a seat, and the guard stood behind her.

The pastor cleared his throat, then spoke in a loud voice. "Good afternoon, everyone. We're here to review the petition to grant early parole to Olivia Stewart. This hearing is in session. Mr. Hopkins, you may begin."

As the stenographer began typing, Keren glanced at her mom. She sat with her back straight and legs crossed at the ankles and tucked to the side, under the chair. Her eyes stared straightforward. Keren saw her jaw muscles flex. It was the only thing that gave away how nervous she felt. This must be terrifying. Either she'd walk away free or the parole board would send her back to prison.

Theodore stood. "Yes, sir. We believe because of Olivia Stewart's cooperation during the Dark Guild trials and her exemplary behavior, she's earned parole." He flipped the page. "I'd also like to point out that her sentence of five years without parole goes against preestablished court precedent. If you look at addendum two, you'll see the references."

All the board members flipped the page, then silence filled the room as they read the document. After a few moments, the pastor spoke.

"Does anyone have questions regarding the petition?" Pastor Declan asked.

"No," each of the members replied.

"Thank you, Mr. Hopkins. You may take a seat." The pastor looked at Keren.

"We'll move to the testimony of the sponsor, Keren Stewart. Please stand and address the parole board."

Emotion churned inside Keren. What if they'd be able to tell she was lying? "I'm here to request the release of my mom, Olivia Stewart, on parole under my sponsorship." Keren heard herself speaking, but her mind screamed for her to stop. "I have an established home and job in Las Vegas and can provide for her there." Lies, all lies. Sweat trickled down her back. "My employer has agreed to employ my mom."

A heavyset blonde woman spoke up. "It says your employer is Calypso Rose. Doesn't he own casinos?"

"Yes, that's correct." Finally, she spoke about something that was true.

The woman's eyebrows went up. "Do you think it's a good idea for an ex-convict to work in a casino?"

Keren took a breath to calm her nerves before answering. "He plans to employ her as his household staff, not in the casino."

The woman puckered her lips and nodded.

A wolf shifter with a scar on the back of his hand rubbed his chin. He'd left the top button of his white too-tight, long-sleeved dress shirt undone, and his tie knot was messy and pulled below the top button. Keren got the impression he'd borrowed the clothes from a smaller-framed friend. He must be the ex-convict, she thought.

"You're telling me a dragon would willingly employ a sorcerer and allow her into his home?" He sat back and gave a crooked smile. "I doubt that."

Keren frowned, annoyance bubbling in her chest. "I'm a sorcerer. Calypso and I have no problem working together."

The ex-convict's eyes widened, as well as several other board members'. A mousey-haired woman leaned over and whispered something into another board member's ear.

"If you have something to say," the pastor said, "say it out loud so it will be in the hearing records. Otherwise, keep silent."

The mousey-haired woman who'd been caught whispering spoke. "I said I wasn't aware Keren Stewart was a sorcerer."

Theodore responded, "That's irrelevant to this hearing."

The pastor flipped through the petition pages. "Let's take a moment to explore this." When satisfied there was no mention of Keren's sorcerer abilities, he looked at Theodore. "Why would you leave that out of the petition?"

"As I stated, it's irrelevant to this hearing." Theodore's voice betrayed a hint of frustration.

"I disagree, Mr. Hopkins," Pastor Declan said. "It is extremely relevant. We have to know if Keren Stewart has, or had, any connections to the Dark Guild. We can't have Olivia Stewart exposed to temptations."

Keren's heart pounded, and she clenched her fists to keep from rushing over and punching the pastor in the face. She shot to her feet, tired of being talked about like she wasn't in the room.

"Of course I had something to do with the Dark Guild. Don't you read the news?"

Pastor Declan's eyes widened, and the mousey-haired woman's mouth fell open. One side of the ex-convict's mouth curled into a smile as he leaned back and rested his hands on his paunch. Theodore put a hand on her leg, but Keren wouldn't be silenced.

"I stopped the cursed creatures that were threatening Orlando and the shifter races. I took the Amplification Disk artifact from Quinlin Turner. It's because of me you have him secured in prison for the rest of his life." Keren looked over at her mom. Tears brimmed in her mom's eyes as she stared back at Keren.

Keren took a deep breath to control the anger churning in her chest. "I put my mom's life in danger. Quinlin kidnapped her and tried to kill her on multiple occasions." Keren looked at Pastor Declan and blurted out, "Whatever interactions my mom had with the Dark Guild were to protect me. I owe her my life." Finally, her honest feelings about her mom had come to the surface. She'd been afraid to face the feeling of guilt. Guilt from knowing her mom had dedicated her life to protect her children from the Dark Guild. She took a ragged breath. "She's helped put countless members of the Dark Guild behind bars." Keren's shoulders lifted with the weight of that deeply buried feeling now revealed. "Give me the chance to make it up to her. We are the two least likely people in the entire world to be involved with the Dark Guild again in our lives."

Pastor Declan shifted in his seat and self-consciously straighten the papers in front of him. "I appreciate your honesty, Keren. Do you have anything else to say before we move to Olivia Stewart's statement?"

Keren shook her head as she sat. "No, thank you. I'm sorry I lost my temper. Please don't hold that against my mom."

Theodore reached over to take Keren's hand and give it a squeeze. His warm hand felt comforting against Keren's clammy skin.

"Olivia Stewart," Pastor Declan said. "Please give us your statement."

The world seemed to move in slow motion as Keren watched her mom stand up and adjust her suit jacket. She lifted her chin and looked each of the board members in the eye. Her mom had given many school and peer lectures and solicited for research funding from intimidatingly wealthy and powerful organizations. She knew how to command a room.

Time caught up as her mom spoke in a clear, confident voice.

"I understand that allowing myself to get involved with the Dark Guild was wrong. I'll regret those actions for the rest of my life." She paused and looked at each board member again. "I have done everything in my power to make amends for my actions and will continue to be an advocate against the Dark Guild and everything they stand for." She looked over at Keren and smiled. This time, her smile extended into her eyes.

Keren's heart melted. Even after everything that had happened, her mom still loved her.

Olivia turned back to the board and somehow looked more confident than before. "I have a great deal to make up for with my daughter. I'm humbled and grateful she's stepped up as my sponsor." Her voice faltered, then she cleared her throat. "I'm capable and willing to work toward being an outstanding citizen once again." She sat down and placed her hands in her lap.

"Thank you, Olivia. I also want to thank Keren, Mr. Hopkins, and the board for their time." Pastor Declan stood. The other parole board members followed suit. "The board will deliberate on the petition. I declare the hearing adjourned." He led the group to a door at the back of the room. The stenographer followed behind them.

Theodore grabbed his briefcase and stood. "Let's get something to drink. This could take a while."

"The cafeteria is down the hall on the right," Olivia's guard said. "We'll send someone for you when the verdict comes in."

"Thank you." Theodore guided Keren out of the room. She avoided eye contact with her mom, since it would have turned Keren into a blubbering mess.

Once seated at one of the round metal tables sprinkled around the room, Keren noticed how depressed and gloomy this cafeteria felt. Two tiny barred windows close to the ceiling were the only natural light source. The same gray tile covered the floor with what looked like years of dirt and grime. If this space was for visitors, what depressing surroundings did they subject the inmates to? She understood why her mom felt so desperate to be released.

Holding a couple of cups of coffee, Theodore sat down and let out a deep sigh.

"Sorry, they didn't have cream or sugar." He leaned forward. "You handled that perfectly," he said.

Keren sipped her lukewarm coffee and cringed at the bitter taste. "Why didn't you want them to know I'm a sorcerer?"

"It really is irrelevant," he said. He sipped his coffee and smiled as if it were an expensive Columbian blend. He must have pitiful coffee at his office.

"Your mother is a sorcerer, but your father wasn't. They should've known you had a fifty-fifty chance of being a sorcerer." He took another sip of coffee. "I thought about listing the positives of you being a sorcerer, but I didn't want the hearing to focus on that. I wanted them to focus on Olivia."

"What positives?" Keren asked. She pushed her coffee away.

"You'd understand the signs of someone using magic. Since there will be a strict no-magic use injunction on Olivia for the rest of her life, having a sponsor aware of the signs is, to me, a great advantage." He frowned. "Do you want something to eat? There's a vending machine."

Keren's stomach rumbled in response, finally admitting her guilt had eased the vice grip on her stomach. "Yes, thanks. Anything with chocolate."

"Sure. I'll be right back." Theodore stood and went to the vending machines.

Keren swept her fingers through her hair, not caring about exposing her elf ears. This had been a roller-coaster ride of emotions. Regardless of the results, Sirena expected Jewel's curse to be reversed. In order to save Katrina, Keren needed the twisted curse reversed, and she needed to find Itorn.

"Here." Theodore put a bag of chocolate chip cookies and a candy bar on the table. "These looked the best to me."

"Thanks." Keren tore open the package of cookies. Even though they had a dry cardboard taste, she kept popping them into her mouth.

Theodore looked at his watch. "If we go past an hour, I consider that a good sign."

"A good sign?" Keren asked after swallowing her mouthful of tasteless cookies.

"Yes, that means some of the board members are fighting for us."

The cafeteria door opened, and a guard called out, "Keren Stewart and Mr. Hopkins, you're wanted back in the hearing room."

Keren stuffed the remaining cookies and the candy bar into her pocket. "What does it mean when they come to a verdict in less than a half hour?"

Theodore's expression darkened. "Probably nothing good." He sighed and grabbed his briefcase as he stood. "Shall we?"

Keren stood and walked to the door. The disappointment she felt surprised her. After suffering through the past few days as she wondered if getting her mom released was the best plan, she realized she needed her mom. She needed to make up for abandoning her these last few months. Now she wondered if she'd ever get that chance.

When Keren entered the hearing room, she saw her mom sitting in the same composed position. Anyone else looking at her would think she was calm and collected. But Keren noticed her clenched jaw and how her thumbs rubbed against one another. Her mom was frightened and nervous.

The members of the parole board sat at their tables. The ex-convict leaned back in his chair with his arms crossed over his chest. He sported an annoying smirk on his face.

Keren gave him a scowl, then took her seat. The mousey-haired woman fidgeted in her chair. Otherwise, the board's posture and movements gave nothing away.

Pastor Declan stood. "This hearing is officially in session."

The stenographer's fingers danced across his machine's keys.

"Olivia Stewart, please stand for the reading of the parole board's decision."

Keren's mom rubbed her hands on her skirt, then stood. Keren thought she saw her sway a bit.

Pastor Declan cleared his throat, then spoke. "The parole board finds it in the public's interest to deny Olivia Stewart's parole."

Without realizing it, Keren gasped. This wasn't the outcome she'd expected.

"Please escort Olivia Stewart back to prison. I declare this hearing adjourned."

Keren jumped from her seat. "No!"

Theodore grabbed her arm, but Keren yanked it free. "Why? Why won't you grant her parole?"

"Keren, you're out of line." The pastor stood, then leaned on the table.

"At least tell us why. You owe us that much!" Keren shouted.

The pastor lowered his head and sighed. When he looked up, he said, "Given the state of affairs in the world, how could you possibly expect us to release her?"

Keren's heart pounded in her chest. The magic frenzy she'd caused was the reason they had denied her mom's parole. She stood with her mouth open but couldn't say anything.

"We'll reassess Ms. Stewart's eligibility for a parole hearing in another six months," the pastor said, then he stood straight and picked up his papers. "I'm sorry. That's the best we can do." The remaining board members stood and filed out the rear door, with the stenographer following behind.

Keren looked at her mom, who was being handcuffed by the guard. "I'm so sorry."

"It's not your fault. I appreciate your trying." Her mom gave a faint smile and let the guard lead her out of the room.

But it was her fault. Magic frenzy had caused the world to fear the magic races, wiping out the hard work they'd made toward acceptance and an amicable existence.

After the guard left with her mom, Keren stood and stared at the closed door. So much had depended on her mom's release. A feeling of dread passed over her. What would Sirena do? Keren would have to think of another plan before she told her about the parole board's decision. When Theodore spoke, it startled out of her thoughts.

"The invitation stands." He stepped closer to her and spoke in a low tone. "At least hear him out."

A chill ran down Keren's spine. The thought of seeing Quinlin again made her sick to her stomach. Gaines might know a sorcerer who would help her. But they wouldn't have experience with curses. How could she trust a stranger with something so important?

She lifted her chin. Just like her mom, she'd do whatever it took to make things right. "Alright, I'll visit."

CHAPTER ELEVEN

KEREN

Security checks were even more stringent for visiting Quinlin. It had taken over an hour for Keren and Theodore to be cleared. She was searched twice and at one point was certain a strip search would be required, but Theodore had intervened.

"You're a sorcerer," the guard stated to Keren.

His round face, oversized lower lip, and pug nose reminded Keren of an orangutang. The round paunch drooping over his belt added to the image. Buttons at the bottom of his shirt strained to contain his girth while exposing a view of his hairy belly.

Keren lifted her eyes and tried to erase the image. "Yes, that's correct."

"You understand this building blocks all magic, both elemental magic and spells?" The guard squinted at her.

Keren nodded. "Yes. I won't need to use my magic."

The guard squinted again, as if he had a superpower that could detect lies. "Any suspected attempt to use magic will get you arrested." He smiled. "Maybe you and Turner can be cellmates."

Theodore cleared his throat. "Are we set to proceed? I don't want to keep my client waiting all day."

The guard pursed his lips, obviously trying to hold back another sarcastic jab. He turned. "This way."

After moving through several locked doors, the guard led them into a visitation room. This wasn't like her mom's visit. This room had a thick glass wall separating two areas. One metal table and two chairs were on each side. Speakers hung from the ceiling on both sides.

"You'll place your hands on the table," the guard said, "the entire time you're inside." The guard eyed Theodore. "Any hand movement will stop the visit." He sneered at Keren. "Or get you arrested."

"If this building blocks all magic, why this strict rule?" Keren asked, tired of this snarky guard.

"Precautions. Technology is fast-paced. You never know when someone might discover a way around security." He pointed a chubby finger to one chair. "Sit."

Keren glared at him a moment before taking a seat. She set both of her hands on the table in the handprint outlines. A chilling cold seeped into her body.

"Good thing I don't talk with my hands," she said as Theodore sat next to her.

"Turner will be in shortly." The guard stood in the doorway. "I'll be right outside." He closed and locked the door.

Keren glanced at the empty hand marks in front of Theodore. "You don't have to put your hands on the table? You're a sorcerer too."

"No. Since I'm Mr. Turner's lawyer, I'm exempt from the rule. Legal requirements also force all recordings of this conversation to stop." Theodore opened his briefcase. "Video, however, is still running. The camera is directly on my back. They can't see my mouth, so they don't know what I'm saying." He pretended to rifle through some papers. "Move your mouth like you're talking to me. If you have to say something, make it nonsensical."

Keren did as instructed. She moved her mouth but only spoke every third or fourth time. "Don't. Understand."

Theodore chuckled. "I just like to mess with them. The law prevents them from videotaping my mouth or Quinlin's." He raised an eyebrow and glanced at her. "Yours is a different story."

She shifted her seat so her back was as much to the camera as possible without taking her hands off the table.

A door opened on the other side, and a tall, broad-shouldered guard led Quinlin in. Quinlin looked terrible. He'd lost at least twenty pounds, and it looked like a crayon box had exploded at close range with the multiple hues of old and new bruises splattered on his face.

Keren's stomach clenched when he gave her his signature smile. This was a bad idea. Every part of her body screamed at her to leave. But she was here now, so she might as well hear him out.

The guard shoved Quinlin into the rickety seat and secured his shackled hands to the metal table. Then, without a word, the guard left.

"Good to see you, Theodore," Quinlin said.

"Yes, Mr. Turner. As you requested, I've brought Keren for a visit."

Quinlin's eyes moved to Keren. She felt dirty as his eyes checked her out. "We have an agreement, then?"

"I'm here to talk," Keren blurted out. She twisted in her seat to block the camera's view of her face.

"My mom didn't make parole." She lifted her chin. Now that she was talking, she was growing more confident. Knowing Quinlin couldn't use magic and having the thick, clear barrier between them helped. "Theodore mentioned you might help me."

Quinlin raised an eyebrow. "I'd love to help." He pulled on his chains. "But I'm unavailable at the moment."

"I want names of sorcerers with expertise in curses who can potentially help me." Keren's sweaty hands felt slippery on the metal table. She pressed them down to keep them in place.

Quinlin sat back. He squinted at Keren. "I've given all the names of my associates to the inquisitors."

Keren stared into his baby blue eyes. Her stomach turned. "I don't believe that for a moment."

One side of his mouth threatened to smile, but Quinlin kept his features neutral. "Let's entertain this request. Say, hypothetically, I come up with names. What do I get?"

"You get nothing," Keren said.

Quinlin shook his head. "That's not how this works. I'm the only one who can help you." He leaned closer. "And you are the only one who can help me." An evil glint flashed in his eyes. "I want out of this hellhole."

Keren's heart raced. "Even if I could, I would never." She didn't want to say the word escape with cameras watching her every move. "There must be something else you need."

"I need my freedom." Quinlin's voice took on an eerie, threatening tone. "The freedom you and Briggs stole from me."

Keren's mouth went dry. She could barely hear him over the pounding in her head. "Tell me what you want, Quinlin."

"I told you. I want out," he smiled. "And I want my Amplification Disk."

Suddenly, Keren's heart stopped. It would be easier to walk out of the prison right now with Quinlin on her arm than convince Calypso to give up the artifact.

"I think we're through here," Keren said.

"For now," Quinlin said. "But you'll be back. I'm your only hope." He smiled at Keren. "How desperate are you?"

Sweat poured down Keren's back. Quinlin was an evil monster. What was she thinking coming here? "Get me out, now!" Keren yelled.

Theodore jumped up and knocked on the door to summon the guard.

After the guard opened the door, he nodded at Keren. "You can take your hands off the table." He stepped back and opened the door wider. "This way."

Keren wiped her palms on her jeans, then clenched and unclenched her hands into fists to get the circulation going. Her body trembled. She was so close yet so far from saving Katrina and the shifter races.

Keren's head spun as she walked out of the prison.

Once she was back in the car and headed to Las Vegas, Keren calmed herself down and tried to think logically, instead of emotionally, about her situation. She hated Quinlin, but she knew beyond any doubt he could reverse the curses. But breaking him out of prison would have to be her last resort.

"Theodore," she said. "Is there any way we can get Quinlin paroled?"

"Absolutely none," he said. "He's not eligible for parole. Besides, if by some miracle they ever released him, they'd never allow him to use magic again."

Legally, thought Keren. Her mind spun with ideas. Quinlin was never one to stay within the law.

"You can take as much time as you need to decide on whether you'll help Quinlin in return for reversing your curses. He has nothing but time."

Keren knew that was a jab at her pressing situation. "I can get another sorcerer to help me."

The lawyer gave her a side-glance as he pulled onto the highway. "You'd trust a stranger?"

"I have no other choice," she said.

"Yes, you do. You're just not willing to admit it yet." He let out a deep breath. "When you're ready to talk, you know my number."

"I'm calling Briggs," Keren said as she pulled out her phone.

Theodore tightened his grip on the steering wheel. "I recommend against getting Briggs involved."

"Don't worry. I don't want Briggs involved with Quinlin." She dialed his number and tapped her finger on her leg as she listened to the ring. "He can help me find another sorcerer."

"Keren?" Briggs sounded agitated. "What's taking so long? How'd the hearing go?"

She squeezed her eyes shut. "Not well. The board denied Mom's parole."

Her mom's grief-stricken face flashed in her mind. Keren vowed she would find Shawn. Then they'd appeal the parole board's decision. They'd get her mom released. But the next possible parole hearing was in six months. She couldn't rely on her mom to help with Jewel or the twisted curse.

"I'm sorry," he said. "I know you were counting on her help. Now that Shawn can take her case back, I'm sure he'll get her paroled. He's a great lawyer."

"Thanks," Keren said.

"I have good news." Briggs's voice lightened.

"What is it?"

"The chief agreed to my special request to send the evidence to Calypso's place overnight. Normally, he'd ship evidence to an inquisitor's station. But I didn't want anyone else knowing we had the documents."

Finally, something was going her way. "That's great. Thank you so much. I know it couldn't have been easy." She took a deep breath and assured herself this was a sign that her luck was changing. "I won't give up on Mom's release, but we won't be able to arrange another hearing in time for her to help. Sirena's already on the verge of joining the merfolk in a war against the sorcerers. Are there any sorcerer inquisitors?" Keren asked. "Maybe they can help."

"No, not that I know of. Hmm."

She smiled, picturing Briggs with his thinking face on with slightly furrowed brows and pursed lips.

"I'll tell you what," he said. "I'll search the case database and pull a list of sorcerers who have worked with inquisitors in the past. I'm sure one or more of them would help."

"That's a great idea." Keren knew Briggs would come up with something.

"I'm in my office. Just give me a minute."

She heard paper shuffling and then the sounds of typing as she waited in anticipation. This could be the answer.

"I can refine the search by security level. I'll pull only the top two tiers." More typing. "OK, I emailed the list to you."

Keren opened her email app. "Yep, I've got it. Thanks. You're a lifesaver. I'll start calling them right away."

"I can help once I get back to Calypso's," Briggs said. "Stay positive. We'll find someone."

Her heart fluttered. She could always count on Briggs. "OK. I love you."

"I love you too."

She hung up and focused on her phone. When Keren opened the attachment in Briggs's email, she saw twenty names and phone numbers.

With her hopes high, she dialed the first number. Paul Samuel sounded like a friendly name.

"Hello?" a deep voice said.

"Is Paul available?" Keren asked.

"Speaking. Who is this?" Paul asked.

"My name is Keren Stewart. I got your name from Commander Wilson. You've helped with inquisitor cases in the past."

The voice sounded guarded. "What do you want?"

"I have a ..." What was she supposed to call this? "A case that I need a sorcerer for."

"What kind of case? And why isn't Commander Wilson calling me instead of you?" He sounded annoyed.

"Commander Wilson is out of town and asked me to call. We need a sorcerer with knowledge of curses."

"Curses? I know nothing about curses. I can't help you."

"Are you sure?" Keren asked, trying not to sound desperate. "We have research material."

"If this has something to do with the messed up fox shifters, I want no part of it."

"No. It's not related at all," Keren said.

"And no curses," Paul said. "That's Dark Guild magic. I'm sorry. I can't help you. Don't call me again."

He hung up.

Keren's mouth hung open as she stared at the phone.

"No luck?" Theodore asked. She saw him fight back a smile.

"There are plenty more on the list." Keren thought she'd change her tactics and not jump straight into curses.

As she dialed number after number, she got either a "phone disconnected" message or the same response as Paul's. No sorcerer wanted anything to do with curses. After calling two-thirds of the names, she shoved her phone in her pocket and closed her eyes. This was getting her nowhere. The hope she felt moments ago had been squashed like a bug. They rode in silence for the rest of the drive.

Theodore pulled up to Calypso's house. "I'll be expecting your call." He shifted in his seat to face her. "The longer you wait, the more expensive this deal will be. Quinlin's already added in the Amplification Disk."

Keren clenched her jaw and got out of the car. She slammed the door shut with more force than necessary. Then she walked inside to give everyone the bad news.

CHAPTER TWELVE

KEREN

"Hi," Keren said as she walked through the drawing room door. Sirena hopped up from the couch. "I was so worried! You've been gone for hours." She ran over, then stood on her toes to peek over Keren's shoulder. "So, when does your mom get here?"

Keren was direct. "I'm sorry. They denied her parole."

"What!" Sirena shouted as she rubbed her fingers over her forehead. "How could they do such a thing? I knew I should have gone with you. How will we remove Jewel's curse without your mom?"

"Briggs sent me a list of sorcerers who've worked with inquisitors on investigations. I'm going to call them." Keren tried to sound positive, even though she knew the list was useless. "I'm sure one of them will help."

"And what if none of them will help?" Sirena asked, obviously agitated.

Keren winced. "Then I'll try something else." She put her hand on Sirena's shoulder. "I promise I'll remove Jewel's curse."

"But how long will you take?" She glanced back at the vessel sitting on the bar. "Jewel's suffering." Then she looked back at Keren and lowered her voice. "And Father is organizing his fighters. He's grown impatient with my empty promises."

"Try to reason with him. Give me a day or two to get things organized." Keren's headache throbbed down the back of her neck. "If I have to, I'll do it myself. Briggs has arranged for Mom's notes to be here tomorrow." She rubbed the back of her neck. "I can do it. I'm sure."

Sirena frowned. "You said before you couldn't. Now you can? I don't understand."

Keren's reply was sharp. "I'm doing the best I can, Sirena. OK?"

The Elf Princess crossed her arms. "Are you going to help Jewel like you promised or not?"

"Yes, Sirena. Give me some space to think." Keren stepped away. Then she heard Nadria's voice.

"Keren?"

When Keren turned to look at Nadria, an immense sadness swept over her. A once-vibrant, confident woman who'd had no problem rallying demonstrations for magic equality while holding a full-time management job at the Kitty Café stood as a fragile waif in the doorway. Nadria's boney fingers clung to the doorframe to hold herself steady. The dark circles under her eyes exaggerated her chalky complexion. "Did you say the parole board denied your mom's release?"

Keren rushed to her side. "Nadria, what are you doing out of bed?"

Nadria released the doorframe and wrapped her arms around Keren. "I'm so sorry."

Keren let herself melt into Nadria's arms. She felt helpless. Her friends and family were suffering while she floundered to find answers.

"I want to help," Nadria said as she stroked Keren's hair. She stepped back. "We'll figure this out." She turned to Sirena. "Does Jewel have any information? We need to know why a sorcerer thought she needed to be stopped. Has she mentioned anything about a sorcerer threatening her?"

Sirena rolled her eyes at Nadria. "Chinese dragons are the most powerful beings on earth. No one threatens them."

Keren felt Nadria's body tense from Sirena's sharp response.

"OK, maybe she did something to them first?" Nadria asked.

"Jewel keeps repeating they lied to her," Sirena said, a worried look passing over her face. "She's not doing very well. I'm worried about her mental state."

Keren frowned. "What do you mean?"

"She used to say more, but now it's just that phrase, 'they lied,' over and over."

"We will save Jewel, Sirena. Don't lose hope." Keren supported Nadria as they walked to the couch and sat down. This was getting them nowhere. Keren didn't know how long she had until the merfolk and elves declared war on sorcerers. A war would put Katrina in even more danger. Sirena sat on Keren's other side.

As Keren looked at Nadria's fragile body, it amazed her that even in her weakened state, she'd still offered to help. Her friend had stepped up time after time, taking brutal beatings. And Keren continued dragging her into one dangerous situation after another.

First, it was searching for evidence to clear her mom's name, then fighting against the Dark Guild. She had even interrupted Nadria's magic studies and asked Nadria to break her into the Council Library to find information on what had really happened to the dragons at the end of the Dragon War. That's when she'd found *The Dragon War Truth*. She remembered rifling through the old tomes in the archive section during her search.

Keren bolted upright. "That's it!" she yelled.

"That's what?" Sirena asked, her eyes wide.

"Nadria, remember when you helped me get *The Dragon War Truth* from the Council Library?"

Nadria frowned. "Yes."

"Well, while I was looking for it, I ran across a book called *The Creation of Sorcerers*."

"I remember you mentioning it. But I'm not following," Nadria said.

Excitement bubbled in Keren's chest. "Let's go way outside the box here." She twisted in her seat to face Nadria. Yes, this was a long shot, but something in Keren's heart told her this was what she needed. "What if historical data on sorcerers is missing because they haven't always existed?"

Nadria rubbed her arm and shivered. "That is a wild idea."

Keren grabbed the blanket sitting on the arm of the couch and tossed it over Nadria. "We need that book."

Sirena's eyes sparkled. "What's in the book?"

Keren hoped the book might contain information that would give her an advantage over Quinlin. "Answers to our questions about Jewel and why a sorcerer cursed her."

"Then let's go," Sirena said as she sprung to her feet. "Where's the Council Library?"

"It's in the Magic Underground," Keren said.

"How do we get there?" Sirena asked.

"There's a portal from Perfect Potions." Keren bit her lip. Even before Nadria had fully recovered, Keren was planning to ask for her help again. "But they only allow Council members and students inside the library."

Nadria took a deep breath and patted Keren's leg. "I'll get you inside."

Keren thought she might be able to use Three to bust down the library's walls. But she really didn't want to destroy the building.

With a heavy heart, Keren took Nadria's hand. "Are you sure you're strong enough?"

Nadria lifted her chin and sat straighter. "I have to be."

Keren squeezed Nadria's hand in thanks, then said, "Alright. We'll ask Calypso if we can use his jet to fly to Orlando tonight."

During the long plane ride from Las Vegas to Orlando, Keren caught a couple of hours of sleep. As the plane's wheels touched the ground, her heart leapt at being back home.

Briggs wanted to come along, but he had to wait for the courier to deliver her mom's notes. The chief inquisitor in Orlando had insisted that only Briggs could sign for the package.

As the plane came to a stop, the flight attendant opened the door and wished them a good day. He said the jet would wait here for whenever they returned.

As Keren stepped out of the jet, she saw a shiny, black limousine waiting for them on the tarmac. The driver stood beside the limousine's open back door. He wore the stereotypical black hat, suit, and tie. His white shirt cuffs showed at the bottom of his jacket sleeves. She could definitely get used to this lifestyle.

Keren, Sirena, Nadria, and Ordell walked toward the limousine. Her friends climbed into the back.

"We're going to Church Street Station," Keren said as the driver opened the front passenger door for her.

"Yes, ma'am," the driver said. He pinched the visor of his hat with his thumb and index finger and gave Keren a nod.

As the limousine pulled away from the jet and began its journey to Church Street Station, Keren watched the familiar landscape pass by. It felt like forever since she'd been here. She turned to face the others.

"Nadria and I will go into the Magic Underground and get the book from the Council Library. You two can wait for us in Perfect Potions."

Keren saw Nadria's mouth twitch as her hand drifted to her necklace, the one that had belonged to Azalea. Nadria had been a star pupil of Azalea's, and the two had formed a close bond.

When the limousine dropped them off in the parking lot, Keren positioned herself next to Nadria. They had a short walk down Church Street to get to Perfect Potions.

"Are you up to this?" Keren asked.

Nadria took Keren's hand and gave it a squeeze. "Yeah. I think so."

Nadria's face was pale. Keren hoped she wasn't pushing her friend too far.

"I can go in alone," Keren said.

"No. You need me to enter the library." Nadria smiled. "Besides, I'd like to check in with my shifter friends to see how they're doing since the magic frenzy cure. I'll have time to do that, right?"

No, was Keren's immediate thought. But she knew Nadria needed this to ground herself.

"Sure," Keren said.

When they entered Perfect Potions, Keren took a deep breath. The smell of lilacs rinsed a wave of calm over her body. Everything looked the same. Purple velvet drapes gave the room a high-class feel. Ornate antique chairs with the same purple velvet sat around several round tables that were scattered throughout the room.

"Hello," a perky voice said.

Keren turned toward the counter. A young fairy with long, curly black hair framing his ridiculously attractive cherubic face stared back at Keren.

"Welcome to Perfect Potions," he said with a beaming smile. He tipped his head. "I remember you. You're Azalea's friends, Nadria and Keren" Then he glanced at Sirena and Ordell. "I don't remember you." He came out from behind the counter. "I'm Farlin." He held his hand out to Sirena.

Sirena lifted her chin but didn't take Farlin's hand. "I'm the Elf Princess."

"Oh." Farlin blinked. Then he gave a slight bow. "Welcome, Your Royal Highness."

Ordell reached out and took Farlin's hand. "I'm Ordell. Nice to meet you." Ordell shuffled his feet. "I'm sorry about Azalea."

"Yes." Farlin's smile faded. "It was a tragedy. This," he motioned around the store, "was her love. I can still feel her presence."

Keren heard Nadria sniffle, and she put her arm around Nadria's shoulder.

"I'm glad to see the store's still open," Nadria said.

"Azalea left the store to me in her will. It shocked me when I learned about it." Farlin looked around the room. "I promised myself I'd keep Azalea's dream alive." He blinked, then flashed his gleaming smile. "What can I help you with today?"

Keren smiled back. Azalea had made a good choice leaving the store for Farlin.

"We're here to enter the Magic Underground," Nadria said.

"All of you?" Farlin's eyebrows went up.

"No, only Keren and me."

"And me!" Sirena shouted.

Nadria looked at Keren, her eyes pleading for a no. Nadria had been acting cordially toward Sirena, but Keren could tell the teenager got under her skin.

"I want to go," Sirena said in a sterner voice. "Jewel's life is in danger."

Keren sighed. "I don't see why you shouldn't. You have elf blood." She pointed at Sirena. "But stay with us. Don't wander off."

Sirena rolled her eyes but didn't object.

Keren looked at Ordell as his face drooped to the floor.

"We can't leave you here alone. Do you want to come along?" she asked.

Ordell looked up at her and smiled. Then he went to Nadria and gave her a hug. "I want to stay with Nadria."

Keren turned to Farlin and shrugged. "I guess we're all going after all."

Farlin gestured toward the counter and the entrance to the back room. "Very good. This way."

Plush runners covering the polished hardwood floor muffled their footsteps as Keren led them to Azalea's office—or what used to be Azalea's office. She couldn't get used to Azalea being gone.

When Keren walked into the office, it disappointed her to see that Farlin had replaced the 1920s decor with a rustic, Western style. A long-horn cattle skull with intricate carvings hung on one wall. Three-tier wood shelves with barbed wire lining the sides hung on the wall beneath two horseshoes. From the ceiling hung a wagon-wheel chandelier. The only thing remaining of Azalea's was the large round mirror encircled with vintage light bulbs.

"Are those deer legs?" Ordell asked as he pointed to a table lamp.

Farlin chuckled. "I had everything manufactured." He held up both palms. "I don't believe in trophy hunting, but I have a fascination for the old West."

"I like the look," Keren said.

"Thanks." Farlin sighed. "I put Azalea's things in storage. She had no relatives." He shook his head, then beamed his Academy Award—winning smile. "Maybe you'd like to look through it? I'm sure she'd be happy to have you take something."

Memories of Azalea's sacrifice during their escape from the goblins had tears brimming in Keren's eyes. Having a memento of her would be nice. Maybe her mom would want something in remembrance of Azalea. "I'd like that, thanks." Keren said.

"No problem. Let me know a few days in advance so I can plan to have someone watch the store." He waved a hand. "Come on, let's get you on your way." Farlin walked across the room and touched the vintage mirror. The surface rippled like a pond that he had thrown a pebble into. When the ripples cleared, Keren saw several shelves of colored glass bottles. Farlin picked four of them up. "Here you go. Should I wait here for you?"

"No, we'll be fine." Keren saw Nadria clutching her necklace, then Keren took three of the glasses from Farlin. "Nadria's necklace is a portal glass."

"Oh, I see." Farlin pointed to Nadria's clamped fist. "May I?"

Nadria loosened her grip on the necklace so Farlin could look at it.

"Azalea's necklace," he said. "It looks lovely on you."

Nadria blushed. "Thanks." She looked down. "I really miss her."

"We all do," he said. "But she's always with us. In spirit."

Nadria nodded and wiped a tear from her face.

"Let's get going," Keren said as she blinked away her own tears. She walked toward the far wall.

She felt Sirena's hand slip into hers. Keren gave it a squeeze, and they all stepped through the door to the Magic Underground.

Keren's heart sank when she emerged into the Magic Underground. The once-beautiful cottages appeared abandoned and neglected. Torn roof shingles littered the ground. Trampled gardens and smashed flower boxes lay in piles of mud. Someone had smeared what looked like tar across the once-vibrant cottage walls. Wisps of smoke drifted from the smashed windows.

"What happened?" Nadria asked. She put a hand on her forehead as she canvassed the devastation. "These poor people."

"It looks like a war zone," Ordell said.

A young bear shifter pointed at Nadria, screamed, then ran the other way. "Fox shifter!" he shouted.

He ran into the arms of an adult wolf shifter who tried to soothe the child's fear. She gave Nadria a nasty look.

Everyone on the street turned to look at them. Some scurried away, while a few others waited to see what would happen. Keren heard doors and shutters slamming shut.

"Get out!" the wolf shifter shouted. "You don't belong here!"

Keren held up her hands. "Wait. I cured magic frenzy. You have nothing to fear from fox shifters."

"Why should we believe you?" the wolf shifter asked.

"Let us help you." Nadria reached out her hand. "We can help rebuild."

"You? Help us rebuild?" The wolf shifter snorted a laugh. "Who do you think caused this turmoil? We want no help from fox shifters."

Nadria shook her head. "Magic races should unite, not divide. We're stronger together."

"You're not welcome here," the wolf shifter snarled.

Jeers and grumbles came from other shifters loitering nearby.

When Nadria started shaking, Keren wrapped her arm protectively around her friend.

"Nadria," Keren said in a low voice. "Don't provoke them. Eventually, they will come to forgive the fox shifters. Right now, let's just get to the Council Library."

Ordell stepped up to Nadria's other side. "Don't worry, Nadria. We have your back."

"Let's go," Keren said as she led the group the short distance to the library. Luckily, the shifters decided not to follow them, and they didn't see anyone else on the way.

As they approached the Council Library, Keren noticed scorch marks on the outside, but it otherwise looked intact.

"Where's the door?" Sirena asked.

"We create one with magic, or, if I have to, I can summon Three." Keren turned to Nadria. "Can you open a door?"

Nadria held her palm up. "I can feel the magic." She scrunched her nose, then nodded. "I think I can still create a door."

Keren let out a sigh of relief. The shifters in the Underground were already on edge. Having Three pummel down a wall would only stir up more hostility.

"Here," Nadria said. "This is the closest entrance to the archives."

Nadria pressed her palm to the wall and furrowed her brow, focusing her attention. The solid rock shimmered, then turned into a wooden door. The group slipped inside and closed the door behind them.

Keren allowed her eyes a few seconds to adjust to the dim light, then she hurried toward the circular tower of books in the center of the building.

"It smells in here," Sirena said.

"They're called books," Ordell said. Then, under his breath, he muttered, "You should read one sometime."

Keren held her breath as she waited for Sirena's reproach, but she must not have heard Ordell's scathing comment.

Keren led them through the maze of tables and chairs filling the room. The last time she and Nadria were here, they kept quiet. But Keren had no time for that now. She knew exactly what she wanted and where it was at.

Keren looked over her shoulder, then waved a hand. "Come on. Keep up." When she reached the twelve-shelf-high column of books, she paused at a door.

"What's the rush?" Sirena asked as she trotted to catch up to Keren.

Keren pushed through the door and waved everyone in. "I want to be in and out before the caretaker notices us." She grabbed Sirena's wrist. "Inside."

"Who's the caretaker?" Sirena asked as she fought against Keren's pull.

Nadria squeezed past Sirena. "He's a phantom fairy who's bound to the library with magic. He's like a guardian of the books."

Sirena pulled her wrist free from Keren and wrapped her arms around her stomach. "Is he dangerous?"

"Only when someone breaks the library rules." Nadria looked at Sirena and lowered her voice as if she were telling a ghost story. "He'll invade the rule-breaker's mind and drive them insane."

Sirena's eyes widened.

"Nadria, stop," Keren whispered.

As Ordell stepped inside, he tipped his head back and pointed up the wrought-iron spiral staircase. "Whoa, this has three floors? I'd like to spend some time here."

Keren tugged on Ordell's sleeve. "There's no time now. We're avoiding the caretaker, remember?" She pointed at the stairs. "We'll make a run for it. Nadria first, then you, then Sirena. I'll bring up the rear."

Keren thought of her creatures. First One appeared in a misty form, then Two, then Three. As she waited for Four, her heart broke with the realization that Four was really gone.

"Keep the caretaker busy while we get the book," Keren said.

"Who are you talking to?" Sirena asked.

"My creatures," Keren said. "They appear to me without my magic. I always thought of them as invisible friends before I knew I could summon them into this realm."

A *bang* made Keren jump, and she looked up at the top of the stairs. The caretaker floated toward them. The phantom fairy stopped and hovered by the second floor railing. He lifted his arm, then slammed his hand down on the railing with a *bang*. Two's and Three's misty forms appeared next to the caretaker. Then Two charged at the phantom. The caretaker moved back, looking unsure what to make of these creatures.

"Go!" Keren shouted.

Nadria moved with as much speed as she could muster. She reached the top of the stairs and rushed down a hallway, skidding to a stop by the locked-off archive section. She waved her hand over the lock, and it opened.

"I'll be right back," Keren said as she bolted to the back of the archive section.

The stuffy air had her fighting back a sneeze. Light from the hallway seemed afraid to reach this back section. She pulled her phone out of her pocket to use the camera light. While running her fingers along the books' spines, she read the titles out loud. "*The Truth Behind Shifter Myths*, *Beginnings of Fire Elemental Magic*... Here it is!" she shouted as she pulled *The Creation of Sorcerers* off of the shelf. She stuffed the book and her phone into her backpack.

She almost knocked Sirena down as she shot out of the archives.

"I've got it. Let's go!" Keren shouted.

Nadria led them back down the stairs. Keren saw her creatures taunting the caretaker, taking his attention away from Keren and the others.

Once outside, the four of them plopped down on a step to catch their breath.

When Keren pulled the book out of her bag, Sirena held her hand out. "May I see it?"

Keren handed the book to the mermaid. Sirena opened it and flipped through the pages. Then she paused, and her eyes grew wide. "It's Jewel!" she exclaimed.

Keren leaned over. The page had an illustration of the vessel holding Jewel.

Sirena laughed. "This is it! This will save Jewel!"

Keren took the book and put it in her backpack. "Maybe." This might be too good to be true, she thought. But Keren let a glimmer of hope build in her heart. "Let's get back to Las Vegas." She turned and led her friends back to the gateway to Perfect Potions.

Tomorrow, she'd be ready to deal with Quinlin.

CHAPTER THIRTEEN

QUINLIN

Quinlin stared at the filthy visitation room's plexiglass window. He cringed, thinking about how some of those smears might have gotten there. A shot of pain flashed in his ribs. He drew in a sharp breath and endured it, not wanting to give the guards the satisfaction of knowing this morning's beating had taken a toll on him.

When Theodore had notified him that Keren wanted to see him again, he allowed himself to feel optimistic. Optimistic that he'd get out of this torture chamber. Optimistic that Keren might still have feelings for him. Optimistic that he'd have another chance to fulfill his father's dreams.

The door on the other side of the plexiglass opened. Keren and Theodore stepped inside and took their seats across from him.

Keren set her hands on the table and scooted her chair around so her back was to the camera. "Tell me your plan."

Quinlin's heart skipped a beat. Keren sat with perfect posture in the chair, and her face looked calm. Her fierce, silvery eyes stared at him with authority. They'd make a perfect couple.

"The exercise yard. That's the only way to break out," Quinlin said.

Keren frowned. "It's not guarded?"

"It is. However, the fence surrounding the yard isn't like the Dungeon's walls." Quinlin stopped, wanting to see if Keren could put the pieces together.

"So, it doesn't block magic?" she asked.

Bravo, Keren. "That's correct," Quinlin said.

"It can't be that easy. What other security measures are in place?" she asked

Quinlin's eyes darted to Theodore.

Theodore cleared his throat. "The fencing is extra-thick cording. It covers the entire yard, including the top. They've posted riflemen and shifters along the prison wall to watch the yards."

"It sounds pretty secure to me." Keren looked at Theodore. "How do you propose I get through?"

"With your creatures. You'll attack from the air to distract the wall guards. Then you'll position your other creatures inside the yard. Between the four of them, they should be able to rip a hole in the fencing."

Keren winced, and she looked down at her hands pressed to the tabletop. "I no longer have Four," she said.

When she looked up and saw Quinlin's baffled face, she sighed. "The water-elemental creature. It ..." she paused and took a deep breath. "It died."

Quinlin raised his eyebrows. So, her creatures *could* be killed. He shook his head, as if dismissing this information. "No matter. Three of your creatures can get the job done. The first thing they will do is get me out of the handcuffs. Then I'll be able to use my magic."

"I'd have to be with One, the air-elemental creature, to see where to summon the others."

Quinlin nodded. "That's right."

Keren frowned. "But the guards will focus fire on One."

"Yes," Quinlin said. Now I'll find out how badly she wants those curses reversed, he thought. "But it has the shield. I saw the creature use it in the hospital."

Keren pursed her lips as she stared into his eyes. This was it. This was the moment she committed or walked away. His heart raced in anticipation.

"I need your word. Swear on your father's memory that you will reverse the curses," She lifted her chin, "whether or not I survive."

Quinlin tipped his head. "If you're dead, why reverse the twisted curse?"

He could tell Keren struggled with what to say next. Intrigue and secrets swirled around her. Very interesting.

"You don't need details. Swear to me." She gave him a cold stare, daring him to say no.

Reversing the curses would be child's play. He needed to know Keren's secrets. "I swear on my father's memory." Quinlin returned her cold stare. "The Amplification Disk. It's part of the deal."

"I don't have the artifact." Her fingers clawed the tabletop. "The dragon warlord has it. I can't give it to you."

Quinlin heard his heart pounding in his head. She was so close to helping him escape. He could taste freedom. But if he backed down from his demands, he'd look weak.

"The Amplification Disk, or no deal." Quinlin gave her a smile.

Keren stared down at her hands. Her jaw muscles flexed. At least she was considering the demand.

She looked into Quinlin's eyes. "Only after you reverse the curses."

He leaned forward. "That's unacceptable." He studied her. Keren's concern over the Amplification Disk appeared genuine. Maybe reversing the curse on Jewel would convince the dragon warlord to turn over the Amplification Disk. "But I'm in a generous mood." He smiled at Keren. "I'll remove Jewel's curse. Then you'll give me the artifact. After that, I'll reverse the twisted curse."

Keren shifted in her chair. She glanced at Theodore, then she glared into Quinlin's eyes. "Deal."

CHAPTER FOURTEEN

KEREN

"So, you're going through with this?" Theodore asked.

"I said I would." Keren kept her eyes on Quinlin. "We should move as quickly as possible."

"Agreed." There was a pause before Theodore continued. "I can't help but think you'll somehow double-cross Mr. Turner."

"Why would you think that?" Keren's head snapped in Theodore's direction. She didn't care if the cameras saw her face. "Because he killed hundreds of shifters? Because he kidnapped and tried to kill my mom?" She furrowed her forehead. "Or is it because he tried to kill me and my friends?"

"All of the above," Theodore said. "I'm looking after the welfare of my client."

"I thought I was your client." Keren scowled.

"We completed our prior business contract. My loyalty lies with Mr. Turner." Theodore turned to Quinlin, then back to Keren. "I want to be clear on that point."

"It's very clear." Keren took a few deep breaths. "I can't guarantee this will work." She looked at Quinlin. "You know that, right?"

Quinlin raised an eyebrow. "I know it will work."

With a deep sigh, Keren slouched in her seat. "Once Quinlin's free, what happens then?"

"Your creatures will carry him away from the prison and leave him at a designated location with me. I have a safe house prepared."

"No." Keren shook her head. "I'm not leaving Quinlin once he's out."

"Where could you possibly hide him that the inquisitors won't find?" Theodore asked.

"I have an idea." She sat straighter and glared at Quinlin. "This is not negotiable. You'll stay with me."

Theodore's face darkened. "I'm not comfortable with this."

"I don't care what you're comfortable with," she said. "He made a deal, and I'm not letting him out of my sight until he fulfills that deal."

Theodore opened his mouth to protest, but Quinlin interrupted. "I'm fine with the arrangement." He smiled. "Will Briggs be there to greet me? I'd love a reunion. We have so much to catch up on."

"No," Keren said through gritted teeth. "I'm keeping everyone away from you."

Quinlin smirked. "A secluded lovers' reconciliation. I'd like that."

Keren fumed. Maybe this wasn't a good idea. She couldn't trust Quinlin. Once her creatures were on the news for breaking Quinlin out of prison, she'd never be able to see her friends again.

She had a plan, but she couldn't pull it off alone.

"You tell me when this is going down, and I'll be there." Keren looked at Quinlin. "Don't think about double-crossing me."

Quinlin smiled. "I wouldn't dream of it. Be here tomorrow at 3:45 p.m." His smile faded. "Don't be late."

Keren gave him a terse nod. "Tomorrow it is." She turned to Theodore. "I'm done here."

Theodore stood and knocked on the door to summon the guard. Keren looked back before she walked out of the visitation room. Quinlin sat there with his familiar smug smile. She shivered, then walked out.

CHAPTER FIFTEEN

BRIGGS

Briggs sat on the couch in Calypso's drawing room, sipping a soda. Ordell sat on the other end, engrossed in something on his phone, while Nadria and Sirena had the contents of the evidence box strewn across the floor as they poured over the information.

Briggs kept checking the time. Keren had told him the warden at her mom's prison needed her to make a trip back. She'd vaguely spoken of a legal-document issue as she got into the car with Theodore. Keren interrupted his thoughts when she walked into the drawing room. It could've been the lighting, but she looked like she had a paler complexion.

"Hey, sorry I'm late." She slid onto the floor between Nadria and Sirena.

"Is everything straightened out?" Briggs asked.

"Yeah, just legal stuff we forgot at the hearing." Keren looked up and flashed Briggs a forced smile. "Everything's straight now." She refocused on the evidence.

"Why couldn't Theodore handle it alone?" Nadria said. She sat back on her heels. "We have so much work to do here."

"I know. I'm sorry, but I had to be there," Keren said as she shrugged. Her eyes remained focused on the paperwork. "A notary at the prison had to witness my signature. No big deal."

Nadria frowned, looking like she wanted to ask more questions. Instead, she continued searching through the papers.

Briggs knew the stress of this situation had made Keren more contemplative, but something felt off. Why a notary at the prison? He rubbed his chin. Keren normally gushed her feelings to Nadria. He'd be sure to check in with Keren tonight before bed to be sure she was alright.

Keren pulled a picture from the stack. "Oh my gosh, this is my dad."

"Can I see?" Sirena asked as she peeked over Keren's shoulder. "He was handsome."

"Yeah, he was," Keren said. "Mom told me every girl in school tried to date him."

"Well, he made the right choice," Sirena said.

Keren smiled at her. "I like to think so."

"One day," Sirena continued, "I'm going to find someone and get married."

"So," Keren sat back, looking and acting more like herself, "what kind of man are you looking for?"

"Handsome, of course." Sirena bit her lip. "He obviously has to be OK with me being the Elf Princess."

"So, an elf?" Nadria asked.

Sirena wrinkled her nose. "I don't think so. I want someone who'll just talk to me. I'm not sure an elf can overlook my status."

"A merman?" Ordell asked.

Briggs startled, surprised Ordell had been following the conversation.

"No, I can't see that," Sirena scooted closer to Keren and leaned in. "Don't tell him," she looked around as if someone were spying to gain intel on her husbandly wishes, "but I think Ryota's kinda cute."

Briggs choked on the soda he was drinking.

"Are you alright?" Keren asked as she jumped up and patted his back.

Sirena seemed unaware that her revelation had caused him to choke. She continued. "Do you think dragons cross magic-race lines?"

Briggs set his soda on the floor and cleared his throat. "Isn't Ryota a little old for you?" Briggs asked. "He has been alive for over one hundred years."

"He still looks young. Besides, merfolk have long life spans too." Sirena leaned back, resting her hands on the floor behind her. "My mom and dad loved each other." She pointed to Briggs, then Keren. "You two are happy together. What's wrong with a dragon and a mermaid?"

Briggs's mouth opened, then closed again. He had thoughts on the matter, but any he voiced would make Sirena angry, and he wasn't interested in the wrath of the teenage Elf Princess.

"Maybe you should ask him," Nadria said. "I mean, ask if he's interested in dating you."

Sirena rolled her eyes. "That would seem desperate, don't you think?"

"Not at all," Nadria said. "He might be attracted to you, but too respectful of your position to tell you or do anything about it."

Sirena frowned. "You think so?"

"Nadria," Keren said bluntly. "Stop playing matchmaker." Her eyes met Briggs's, asking for help.

Sirena ignored Keren. "You might be right. He's too respectful to chance overstepping his bounds." She paused and tapped her index finger on her bottom lip. "Where would we go on a date around here?"

"No," Briggs said. "I don't think that's a good idea."

Sirena ignored Briggs, too, as she rubbed her chin. "He could fly us anywhere. Maybe a movie?"

Briggs threw his hands up and flopped back on the couch. His mind spun just thinking about the repercussions of such a duo. Or even worse, if they dated and it broke off badly.

"You're getting sidetracked," Briggs said. "I have to send the evidence back to the station in four days."

Ordell gave a smirk and set his phone aside. "OK, let's get back to work." He leaned toward Sirena and put a hand on her shoulder. "I say go for it."

"Ordell," Keren said. "Stop already."

"Thanks." Sirena lifted her head. "Maybe I will."

Sirena pulled over *The Creation of Sorcerers* and flipped through the pages. By the look on her face, Briggs knew she wasn't reading a word.

"Here," he reached out. "Let me have the book."

Sirena frowned at him. "Why?"

"You're distracted." Briggs wiggled his fingers. "You might miss something important."

Sirena sighed but gave up the book. Then she stood up. "I'm going to get something to eat." Her eyes flicked to Nadria. "I'll be back."

Sirena hurried out of the room.

"Nadria," Keren hissed, "what on earth are you doing?"

Nadria shrugged. "Just trying to help." She gave a sly smile. "Can you imagine those two together?"

"No," Keren said. "I can't."

That conversation continued, but Briggs stopped listening. He focused on the book.

"Hey," he interrupted. "Listen to this."

"What is it?" Keren asked.

"If this book is correct," his fingers followed the words on the page, "a great Chinese dragon granted humans sorcerer abilities."

"That must be about Jewel," Keren said with excitement in her voice. "What else does it say?"

Briggs flipped the page. "It says humans were fearful of being the only race without magic. They lived in terror of annihilation by the magic races." He looked up at Keren. "So the Chinese dragon picked strong human bloodlines and granted them magic."

"How did she do that?" Ordell asked.

Briggs shrugged. "It doesn't say. It's just part of the dragon's magic abilities, I guess."

"What else does it say?" Keren asked.

"When the new sorcerers began using their magic aggressively instead of defensively, as the dragon had intended, she got angry and threatened to take their magic away. To keep that from happening, the sorcerers cast a curse on the dragon."

"I thought sorcerers had always existed, like the other magic races," Ordell said. He frowned. "Maybe that explains Calypso's hatred of sorcerers."

Briggs closed the book. "Calypso hates sorcerers because they imprisoned dragons. But Jewel's curse could be part of it." He handed the book to Keren. "There are some details about the curse. Maybe you and the sorcerer you find to help can make sense of the notes."

Keren's hand trembled as she reached for the book. "Let's hope so. This is the biggest breakthrough so far. Thanks."

Keren seemed nervous, even afraid. Briggs wanted answers to his questions. He hadn't known Keren planned to go to Orlando. If he had, he would have spoken to the chief in person. Instead, he'd had to wait for the courier, alone, at Calypso's. And tonight, this last-minute need to drive to the prison. He couldn't shake the felling something was off.

"Do you want to take a break? Maybe a walk outside?" Briggs asked.

"I just got here." Keren stretched. "But I'm exhausted. A break sounds good." She looked at her phone. "It's past dinnertime. After our walk, we'll stop by the kitchen for food."

At least she hasn't lost her appetite, Briggs thought.

Ordell moved next to Nadria. "A minute ago, you were telling us to hurry. Now you're taking a break after you just got here?"

Briggs stood. "It's just for a minute. You two can continue while we're gone."

"I see how it is," Ordell said. He shuffled his hands through the papers on the floor. "Do as I say, Ordell. You don't need to eat, Ordell." He tried to keep a straight face but let a smile crack through.

Briggs ruffled Ordell's hair. "We'll bring some food back with us." He held out his hand again to Keren. "Come on. We'll only be gone a few minutes."

Keren put her soft hand in his, and chills ran up his arm at her touch. He pulled her into an embrace, then led her out the door. After stepping away from the front door lighting, the darkness engulfed them, whispering a false sense of peace and tranquility.

The crisp air tingled against his skin as he walked. "It's getting colder." He looked at Keren. "Do you need a jacket?"

She shook her head and wrapped her arms around her waist. "No, I'm fine."

Briggs sighed. "I miss Orlando. I wish I could have gone with you."

"Me too." Keren slipped her hand into his. "I'm sorry. This will be over soon."

He turned to face her. "Will it?"

Keren squeezed his hand. "I think so." She stopped and faced him. "Once the twisted curse is reversed, I'll just be a regular old human."

Her face told him she didn't believe the words coming out of her mouth. The stress of Sirena always on her back to free Jewel and the disappointing decision at her mom's hearing had put a lot of pressure on Keren. She needed his support, not his questions.

He wrapped his arms around her. "That suits me just fine. We'll live happily ever after."

She squeezed him. "That's all I want. You, me, Katrina, and Mom. And Nadria and Ordell."

Briggs chuckled. "And Sirena and Ryota."

She pulled back and slapped his arm. "Stop. That's just wrong."

"She's a spitfire," Briggs said. "She'll have Ryota wrapped around her finger before you know it."

"I mean it, Briggs." Keren pushed her index finger into his chest. "Stop encouraging that relationship."

"I'm not encouraging it," he said as he wrapped an arm around her. "You know I'm just teasing."

She laid her head on his shoulder. "Thanks for being there for me."

He kissed the top of her head. "I'm always here for you."

CHAPTER SIXTEEN

KEREN

"I think we should get back inside," Briggs said. "There's a lot left to go through."

Keren patted Briggs's chest. "You go ahead. I'll be there in a few minutes."

Briggs frowned. "Everything alright?"

She shrugged. "Yeah, I just need to clear my head."

Briggs rubbed her arm. "I can stay with you."

She smiled at him. "No, go back inside. You can keep the research moving. I need a few minutes alone."

Briggs couldn't be here for what she had to do next. Lying to him tore at her heart, but she knew it was for his own good.

She laughed. "Besides, Ordell needs his food."

His hand wrapped around the back of her neck, and he pulled her in close. She stood on her tiptoes. As she tipped her head back, anticipating the kiss, Briggs's lips brushed over hers. She leaned into him, but he pulled back, teasing her. Looking into his lavender eyes, she saw his raw, animal desire, his need to be with her. He wrapped his fingers in her hair and pulled her toward him. His desperate lips locked onto hers.

His strong arm clutched her waist, and he lifted her from the ground. Keren wrapped her legs around his waist as she pressed herself into his body. She wanted to melt into him.

"Keren," Briggs panted. He kissed her forehead, then her cheek. When he moved down to her neck, she couldn't help but let out a moan. She put her hand on his chest and gently pushed away. He stopped kissing her neck and rested his forehead on hers.

"Briggs," Keren whispered. "I…"

His arm loosened, and she stepped onto the ground.

Briggs let out a sigh. "When this is over."

"When this is over," Keren repeated.

"Don't be too long." He kissed her palm and walked back into the house.

Once Briggs had closed the door, Keren pulled out her phone and dialed. Her heart pounded while listening to the ring.

"Hello." Calypso said.

"This is Keren."

"I know. I have caller ID."

She ground her teeth. Why was everyone so sarcastic? But she took a deep breath and continued talking. "I need to talk to you and Sirena privately."

"Hmm. I'm at home," Calypso said.

"Good," Keren said. "I'm standing outside on the lawn. I have something critical to discuss."

"Well"—Keren heard the clinking of ice—"I'm intrigued. Are you coming inside?"

"No." Keren looked around the property. She spotted a gardening shed. "Meet me in the shed."

"Keren Stewart," Calypso said in a playful voice, "what are you up to?"

"Shh," Keren hissed. "I don't want anyone to know I'm talking to you."

"Relax, I'm alone."

She heard rustling.

"We'll be there in five minutes."

"How will you get Sirena to come with you?" Keren wished the Elf Princess carried a cell phone.

"I've seen her tagging after Ryota. She'll agree when he tells her it's a good idea."

Ew. Keren shivered. Sirena had been serious about Ryota.

"Thank you," she said. "I'll see you in a few minutes."

She trotted across the well-manicured lawn and had no problem opening the unlocked shed. Calypso should be more careful about his belongings, she thought. But then again, who would steal lawn equipment from a family of dragons? The door creaked when she pushed it open. It was even darker inside, but she didn't want to use her phone light in case someone was watching. She left the door open to let in some light from the moon.

"Where are they?" she muttered under her breath. While hopping in place to keep warm, she worried Briggs might come looking for her if she took too long.

"Keren?" Sirena asked.

Keren let out a sigh of relief. "Yes."

"What in the world are you doing?" The Elf Princess stepped inside the shed. She sniffed the air. "It smells in here."

"Is Calypso with you?"

"I'm here," he said as he stepped into the shed behind Sirena. "This cloak-and-dagger act is unlike you." He pointed to a bag sitting on the floor. "And that smell is manure."

"Gross." Sirena wrinkled her nose. "This better have something to do with Jewel."

"It does." Keren motioned for them to come in. "Close the door."

Keren heard the door click, and the shed fell into total darkness. She jumped when the overhead light turned on. Calypso stood with his hand on the switch. "Does this ruin the mood?"

"I like the light on," Sirena said.

"It's fine." Keren scrubbed her hands over her face. How should she even start this conversation? Being straight forward was always the best choice.

"I need your help to break Quinlin out of prison." She heard her heart pounding. The words felt sour in her mouth.

"The leader-of-the-Dark-Guild Quinlin?" Sirena scrunched her face. "I thought you hated him."

"I do," Keren said.

Sirena's eyes widened. "But he can reverse Jewel's curse!" she yelled.

"Shh." Keren put a finger to her lips. "This has to stay between us. I especially don't want Briggs to know."

Calypso crossed his arms and leaned on the wall. "This is out of character for you, Keren Stewart." He smiled. "I like this change from good girl to lawbreaker."

Keren's face flushed red as doubt crept into her mind. Was this another impulsive decision that would have catastrophic effects?

"Well, tell us more." Sirena's eyes flickered around the shed as she hugged her arms around her waist. "I don't want to be here any longer than I have to."

"I just came from visiting Quinlin. He agreed to reverse both Jewel's curse and the twisted curse if I help him escape from prison." She licked her lips and looked at Calypso. "And I promised him the Amplification Disk."

Calypso's hand shot to the artifact around his neck. "I will never release this back into a sorcerer's hands."

Keren held her hands up. "Here me out."

"No." Calypso reached for the door handle. "You're trying to trick me into getting the dragons imprisoned again."

"I'm not!" Keren shouted. "I want to end sorcerer magic."

All went quiet, as if the entire world were waiting to hear what would happen next.

Finally, Calypso spoke. "Explain what you mean by 'end sorcerer magic.'" His grip tightened on the door handle.

Without hesitation, Keren launched into an explanation. She couldn't lose this sliver of an opportunity Calypso had given her.

"The book we took from the Council Library, *The Creation of Sorcerers*, said Jewel had cast a spell to give normal humans magic. I think they cursed her when she threatened to take it away."

Calypso's hand relaxed and fell from the door handle. "Go on."

Keren's chest fought to contain her pounding heart. She had one shot to convince Calypso to give up the artifact that had devastated the dragon race.

"The deal is, Quinlin reverses Jewel's curse before I give him the Amplification Disk."

Calypso's fingers rubbed over the artifact.

"I get it!" Sirena shouted. "Once Jewel is free, she can take magic from the sorcerers."

Keren nodded. "That's right, Sirena." Keren lifted her chin and looked at Calypso. "But this plan won't work without you, Calypso. I know giving Quinlin the Amplification Disk is dangerous. But it's the only way to set Jewel free, save my sister, and stop sorcerers from attacking shifter races once and for all."

Calypso squinted. "How do you know Jewel can or will take sorcerers' magic?"

"I don't." Keren turned to Sirena. Even in the cold, sweat trickled down her back. Her sister's life depended on a teenage mermaid. "But you can ask her."

Sirena shook her head. "She's so fragile. I'm not sure she'll understand me."

"Without a guarantee from Jewel, I'm afraid I cannot agree with this plan." Calypso reached for the door handle again. "I can't help you."

"Wait!" Keren held up her hand. She couldn't lose Calypso's cooperation. "Sirena said Jewel keeps repeating 'they lied.' She has to be referring to the sorcerers."

Calypso shook his head. "You can't know that."

While pointing at Calypso, Keren lowered her voice. "No. But you can."

When Calypso gave her a puzzled look, her confidence grew.

"You know exactly how she feels because sorcerers also imprisoned you. You could think of nothing else but getting revenge for what happened to you, your family, and your thunder." Keren's breath came in short pants. "I remember you were obsessed. You know Jewel will feel exactly the same. Sorcerers will be lucky if tearing their magic away is the only thing she does to them."

Calypso crossed his arms over his chest. "Alright, I can agree with that argument. How long will it take for Jewel to enact her revenge from the time her curse is reversed?"

"I don't know." Keren shook her head. "But she has to wait until Quinlin reverses the twisted curse. And Quinlin can't know we're planning on taking away sorcerer magic."

"So there will be a time a dangerous sorcerer has possession of the artifact?" Calypso shook his head. "I won't agree to that."

"Isn't the risk worth being free from sorcerer magic forever?" Keren asked.

His jaw muscles flexed. "You ask a great deal."

"Well, prepare yourself. I'm about to ask for more." Keren put her hands on her hips. "I have to use my creatures to break Quinlin out of prison. If everything goes as planned to reverse the twisted curse, this will be the last time I summon them into this realm. I don't want them remembered as outlaws."

"What choice do you have?" Sirena asked.

As Keren put on her best puppy dog eyes and looked pleadingly into Sirena's eyes, she brushed one side of her hair behind her elf ear. "This is where I need your help. I remember the elf soldiers cloaked themselves when they attacked us after we fled from the elf village." She took Sirena's hands. "If elves can cloak my creatures during the prison break, no one would see them."

Sirena blinked. Her hesitation worried Keren. Maybe this was too much of a risk for the Elf Princess.

"And," Keren added, "we'd have the extra forces of your powerful elven army to help."

Calypso shook his head. "The cloak magic won't work in the prison."

"I know. I have a plan." Keren squeezed Sirena's hands. "Will you help me? For Jewel?"

Keren felt a wave of guilt at using Jewel to push Sirena into agreeing, but she needed the elves for this to work.

Sirena sighed. "I'm listening."

CHAPTER SEVENTEEN

QUINLIN

At 3:45 p.m., guards pushed Quinlin into his exercise yard. He walked with a limp because of the beating he'd received earlier that morning. The need for revenge burned through his body. Keren better hold up her end of the bargain, he thought.

He searched the sky but saw no sign of her air-elemental creature. Sweat dripped down his back as the seconds ticked by.

The poor reception in the exercise yard made Quinlin's earpiece crackle, forcing him to strain to understand Theodore's voice. "She *crackle crackle* plans the same *crackle*."

The earpiece had showed up in Quinlin's oatmeal this morning, which probably added to the equipment's struggles. Regardless, he was grateful for Theodore's loyalty and ingenuity.

Suddenly, a fireball came out of nowhere and spread across the top of the guard wall. Guards screamed, and Quinlin saw two of them topple from the wall in a ball of fire.

Sirens went off, and he threw himself to the ground as another fireball surged over his head. He didn't know that Keren's air-elemental creature could breathe fire.

Quinlin rolled over and looked up as the caged roof tore itself free. A growl bellowed through the air, causing the ground to vibrate beneath him. Gunfire sounded all around him. Water-jet streams and fireballs haphazardly danced around the yard. His feet slipped in the sticky mud as he tried to push himself to the side.

The guards were shouting and stomping through the yard. Their rifles waved wildly in the air, searching for a target. But the sky looked clear.

A young guard's panicked, wild eyes darted from side to side. "What's happening?" He pointed his rifle up, sweeping it through the air as he shot into the empty sky.

"We're under attack," an older guard answered. "Keep your weapon under control. We don't want a guard taken down by friendly fire."

An invisible blow struck the two guards, sending them crashing into the far wall. They dropped their rifles and slumped down into the mud.

Quinlin felt a heavy weight on his chest, then powerful hands pulled him upright. His chained feet dangled helplessly above the ground. Hot breath passed over his face as he stared at Keren's earth-elemental creature. It bared its massive canine teeth in a snarl. Quinlin blinked. Where had it come from?

"The prisoner is gone!" a guard shouted.

Next to the creature stood a soldier with a high-powered rifle in his hands. He took aim, and in three quick shots, downed the remaining three guards in the yard.

"Stay close to me," the soldier ordered.

The creature tore the cuffs off of Quinlin's wrists, then dropped him onto the ground at the soldier's feet to take off Quinlin's ankle cuffs. Then the creature disappeared into mist.

Quinlin lifted his head to get a better look at the soldier. He wore a leather breastplate and arm bracers. Pointed ears poked through his long blonde hair.

"Who are you?" Quinlin asked.

"Stand up, stay quiet, and stay close to me so I can cloak you," the soldier ordered. "I'm in Her Majesty the Elf Princess's army. I was ordered to extract you from this location."

Quinlin scrambled to his feet. He rubbed the raw skin around his wrists. He let out a laugh. He was free. "You're an elf?" Quinlin asked.

The soldier scowled at him. "What tipped you off?" He motioned up with his head. "There's our ride."

Quinlin's jaw dropped when he looked up. He saw a dozen dragons circling in the sky above. Each of them had an elf on its back.

"Where did they come from?" Quinlin asked.

"Elves can link their cloaking abilities together. Once you joined my cloak, you could see all the others." The soldier waved an arm in the air.

Six dragons consecutively rained fire down on the prison wall. Shrieks sounded as a guard jumped from the wall and plummeted to the ground.

Quinlin heard pounding footsteps coming from inside the prison. "I hear more guards coming."

The soldier pointed into the air. "Don't worry. Our ride is here."

The red dragon, the largest of them all, swooped down toward them. It barely made it through the hole in the prison yard's caged roof. Its wingspan took up the entire width of the yard. Keren, a golden glow surrounding her, and another elf rode on the dragon's back. The dragon's talons sunk into the muddy yard as it landed.

Keren's air-elemental creature appeared from mist as more guards poured into the yard. The guards took random aim and fired into what, to them, looked like an empty sky. The air-elemental creature swooped down, positioning itself between Quinlin and the guards. The air vibrated around its body, just like it had in the hospital when he had first seen the magnificent creature.

"There," said a guard, pointing at Keren's creature. "We hit something over there."

All the guards focused fire on the spot where the air-elemental creature hovered.

As a stream of fire shot from the red dragon's mouth, the guards shouted and dove to the side. One guard dove too late. He howled as his clothing burst into flames. He frantically ran in a circle, then back into the prison.

A red, scaly tail swung around, practically knocking Quinlin off his feet. "Climb up!" Keren shouted.

Quinlin's chest swelled with pride. Keren had dragon and elf allies.

She held her hand out. "Hurry!" she shouted at him in annoyance.

Quinlin grabbed the tail and scrambled up. He tried to move quickly, but his battered body wasn't cooperating. The elf soldier pushed from behind, helping Quinlin onto the dragon's back.

Quinlin heard the elf soldier grunt as he fell to the ground. One of the prison guard's randomly aimed bullets had hit him.

"Go, Calypso!" Keren shouted.

The dragon spread its wings and jumped into the sky.

Keren's air-elemental creature somersaulted, then took the injured elf soldier into its talons. The creature shot into the air, sailing past them, with the soldier safely in its grip.

Quinlin settled himself behind Keren on the dragon's back. So this was the infamous dragon warlord.

"Hang on!" Keren shouted as more guards ran into the yard.

Quinlin clutched Keren's waist, and the wind blasted his face as the powerful dragon's wings lifted them into the air. He laughed out loud. This was a far better prison escape than he had ever imagined. With the elves out of hiding, he could have them construct multiple Amplification Disks. Or even something more powerful. He had so much work to do.

Quinlin looked down at the guards fading into the distance. Standing in front was the guard who had named him "pretty boy."

He pressed one palm downward. *"Potestatenum."*

His body quivered as the magic surged through him. He'd missed this feeling. The feeling of ultimate power. The energy ball struck its target, obliterating the guard.

Quinlin let out another laugh, then he felt a sharp pain in his neck. He looked forward and saw Keren with a syringe in her hand.

"Sorry, Quinlin. But where we're taking you is confidential."

His protest came out in babbling noises as the world went dark around him.

CHAPTER EIGHTEEN

KEREN

Keren sat on the arm of a light-beige leather chair. Calypso had set Quinlin in the chair over an hour ago. She lightly slapped Quinlin's face twice.

"What was in that syringe?" she asked.

"Just a sedative." Calypso leaned back on the overstuffed leather couch. "He'll come around soon."

Keren stood and faced Calypso. "Thank you, again, for helping."

She looked around at the posh penthouse Calypso had prepared. A glass-top coffee table sat between the leather chair and couch. A six-seat dining room set stood off to the side with an elegant crystal chandelier hanging over the center. Tucked in the corner was a fully stocked bar.

Normally, this penthouse would have an excellent view, but Calypso had covered all the windows from the outside so Quinlin couldn't tell where he was at.

"It is to our mutual benefit." He raised his glass to her and took a sip of the dark liquid.

Hearing Quinlin moan, Keren spun around. She leaned forward. "Quinlin?"

He moaned again and opened his eyes while putting the palm of his hand on his forehead. "What did you do to me?"

"I sedated you," Keren said.

Quinlin blinked his eyes and squinted against the light. "Why?"

Keren crossed her arms and braced herself for an angry outburst. "You're under my house arrest until you've reversed the curses."

"But with much better accommodations," Calypso said. "I've arranged for clean clothes in the master bedroom. You have a fully stocked kitchen and bar. Maid service will be in once a day, and I've arranged for a cook to prepare your evening meals." He took a sip of his drink. "Do you have any allergies or food preferences the cook needs to be aware of?"

Quinlin lifted his head from the back of the chair and stared at Calypso with a bewildered look. "Who are you?"

"Well," Calypso said as he set his drink down and pushed himself off the couch, "I'm Calypso, the dragon warlord of the last remaining thunder of dragons." He walked over to Quinlin and extended his hand. "You must be the notorious Dark Guild leader I've heard so much about."

Quinlin tried to stand but fell to the side.

Keren caught Quinlin's arm and helped him back into the chair. "You should sit down until the sedative wears off completely," she said.

Quinlin nodded, then took Calypso's hand. "I'm Quinlin. I'm sorry I can't stand and greet you properly. Thank you for helping me escape."

"You're welcome." The smile left Calypso's face when Quinlin's eyes locked onto the Amplification Disk hanging around Calypso's neck.

The hair on the back of Keren's neck rose. These two were playing nice, but how long until things erupted into a turbulent storm?

Quinlin released Calypso's hand and pointed to the artifact. "That belongs to me."

"Not yet." Calypso's face hardened. He pointed around the room. "There are multiple cameras and other surveillance equipment positioned throughout this suite. I have dragons posted outside with orders to roast you alive should you try to leave before we give you permission to do so."

Quinlin rubbed the back of his neck. "Is that so?"

"No one knows your location, Quinlin. We'd overpower you if you tried anything stupid." Keren frowned at him. "Not even Theodore knows where we're keeping you."

Quinlin raised an eyebrow. "I'm impressed. It looks like you've gotten the upper hand in our agreement."

"I want you out of my life just as much as you want your freedom," Keren said. She pointed to the dining room table. "I have all my mom's notes from when she worked with Marcus. I also have information on Jewel that might help you reverse her curse."

Quinlin pushed himself up off the chair. He wobbled but kept his footing. "First, I reverse Jewel's curse, then I get the Amplification Disk. That was our agreement."

"Yes," Calypso said. "I will turn the artifact over to you as soon as we verify Jewel's back to normal."

"But until you reverse my twisted curse, you'll stay right here," Keren added.

Quinlin laughed. "You've changed, Keren."

She lifted her chin. "I have changed. You're not taking advantage of me again."

Quinlin looked at Calypso. "That artifact magnifies the power of a sorcerer's spell. What makes you think I won't use it against you once I have it in my possession?"

It was Calypso's turn to laugh. "You could try, but it would fry you into a pile of ash."

Quinlin's face dropped. He must've thought Calypso didn't know how the Amplification Disk worked.

Calypso stepped toward Quinlin. "I was present the first time a sorcerer used the Amplification Disk to imprison the dragon race." His voice lowered. "I saw the artifact's magic burn the sorcerer wielding it from the inside until they disintegrated."

Quinlin's face paled. As much as she enjoyed seeing Calypso put Quinlin in his place, she had to interrupt the tense confrontation.

"We'll leave you to your work." Keren looked at Calypso. "Are you ready to go?"

Calypso stepped back, but his eyes remained fixed on Quinlin's. "You'd better be as good as you claim." He turned and sauntered to the door. With one final glare at Quinlin, he walked out.

Quinlin let out an exasperated huff. "I thought the Dragon War destroyed the dragon race." He looked down at his muddy prison uniform as if just noticing he still had it on. His lip curled as he brushed dirt off his sleeve. "You're telling me the Amplification Disk imprisoned the dragons instead?"

"Yes." Keren felt uncomfortable with this conversation. She didn't want to give Quinlin too much information. "When the artifact went into the elemental realm with my creatures, any spell that a sorcerer had cast with it ended. Which were your cursed creatures and the containment field holding the dragons prisoner."

"Then why would he give it to me?" Quinlin asked. "It makes little sense."

"He wants Jewel freed. It's a promise he made to his brother." Keren put her hands on her hips. "You understand that, right?"

Quinlin tipped his head. "I understand commitment to family."

"Good." Keren pointed at the dining room table. "After you get cleaned up, you can get started. There's a phone on the table. It can only call one number. When you have something to share, let us know." She turned and walked toward the door. Then she turned back to Quinlin. "Do you need Jewel here to reverse the curse?"

Quinlin shook his head. "No. The intended victim of a curse must be present when casting the curse, but a reversal can be done with or without the victim present." He frowned. "Why?"

Keren shrugged. "Just wondering. Jewel's caretaker doesn't enjoy letting her out of her sight. It will be much easier if she doesn't have to come here." At least she didn't have to tell Quinlin about Katrina. She walked out of the penthouse.

Standing guard outside the door was Petrov. The gray-haired dragon gave her a nod as she passed by. She felt sorry for Petrov. When she'd released the dragons from their prison, Petrov's magic hadn't returned, leaving him unable to shift to his dragon form. Calypso told her it was because of his age. She wished there were something she could do to help him.

Keren saw Calypso waiting for her at the elevator, and she hurried over.

He pushed the down button. "He's arrogant," Calypso said. "Do you think he'll do the job?"

It takes one to know one, she thought. "If anyone can, it's Quinlin."

Calypso looked at her. "I'm confident he can. But *will* he do the job?"

"I don't know. He wants the artifact. And he wants his freedom." She walked into the elevator. "But he's good at finding ways around the system."

"Like he figured out how to escape from prison," Calypso said as he hit the lobby button.

"Exactly." Her stomach felt queasy. "You're monitoring him?"

"Yes. Between the PIB and my dragons, we'll know every move he makes." Calypso tilted his head. "Or doesn't make."

Keren frowned. "What do you mean by that?"

"I mean, logically, there are things he should do unconsciously. He just escaped from prison and is in a luxury suite. He should exhibit certain behaviors because of this change."

"You're a psychologist now?" Keren asked.

"I've had a hundred years to study humans. You are, if nothing else, predictable."

She shook her head. "Don't underestimate Quinlin. He's a level of crazy that goes beyond normal human behavior."

"Duly noted," Calypso said. "How long?"

Keren looked at him. "How long for what?"

"How long do we wait for him to finish before we kill him?"

Keren startled. "What do you mean?"

Calypso sighed. "You have so much to learn about this side of the law. Either Quinlin fulfills his end of the bargain or we kill him. There are no other options."

Keren furrowed her brows. She hadn't thought about what to do if Quinlin couldn't, or wouldn't, fulfill his end of the bargain. "We don't have to think about that yet."

"Then how long until we think about it?" Calypso leaned in close. "I'm not known for my patience."

She only had three days until Briggs had to return the evidence. "Give him two days," she said. "Then we'll talk to him."

"Agreed," Calypso said as the elevator doors opened. He motioned for her to step out.

"If he calls, I want to know. Day or night," Keren said. She pulled a phone from her pocket. "This should stay with whomever is monitoring the room."

Startled, she almost dropped the phone when it rang. She opened the phone and clicked the answer button, then put the call on speaker. "Hello?"

Quinlin sounded irritated. "If this is a test, you must think I'm an idiot."

Keren frowned at Calypso. He shrugged his shoulders.

"I'm not following you," Keren said.

"The so-called curse on Jewel," Quinlin snarled.

"Are you saying there's no curse on Jewel?" Keren asked.

"Of course there is. But if these documents you gave me are correct, the curse is rudimentary and was created by some idiot with little to no understanding of magic."

"Does that mean you can reverse the curse?" Keren asked.

"Of course I can," Quinlin barked. "Are you trying to insult me?"

"No." Keren looked at Calypso. "Calypso and I will be right there."

They both hurried back to the elevator.

CHAPTER NINETEEN

QUINLIN

After not being able to resist a quick look at the material Keren had left, Quinlin paced the room with papers crushed in his hand. His skin itched from the prison grime. The stench of his own body made his stomach sour. He moved back to the table and picked up another paper.

"Do they think I'm that stupid?" he muttered out loud. "I could have cast this curse as a child."

He looked closer at the papers. "I'm missing something." He squinted. Keren had become more cunning since their last encounter. She'd photocopied these pages from a book. Why hadn't she given him the entire book?

He turned to the door when it opened. Keren and Calypso rushed in.

Quinlin waved the papers in the air. "These came from a book. I want to see the entire book."

Keren's face flushed with anger. Her silver eyes glared at him. "You said you were ready to reverse Jewel's curse. That's why we came back."

"I said I could reverse Jewel's curse." Quinlin waved the papers in her face. "I want the book."

"That's impossible," Calypso said.

Quinlin pursed his lips. This dragon was getting on his nerves. "Why?"

Calypso put his hands behind his back and circled around to Quinlin's other side. "I burned the entire elders' library."

Quinlin blinked at hearing this unexpected news. The elders' library contained historical information on every sorcerer spell and curse cast. His chest tightened as fury built up in his gut.

"You did what?" Quinlin asked as he stepped toward the dragon warlord.

Calypso stood his ground. He and Quinlin stood toe to toe.

"I burned it to the ground." Calypso motioned to the papers in Quinlin's hand. "I allowed Keren to make copies of those pages for Jewel's sake."

Quinlin stared into Calypso's eyes, looking for the lie. The dragon's face and demeanor didn't betray him.

"That was unwise," Quinlin said in a low voice. "That library contained important information."

Calypso shrugged and stepped away. "To you." He walked behind the bar and poured himself a drink. Holding the bourbon bottle up, he raised his eyebrows.

Quinlin glared at him, unmoving.

Calypso set the bourbon bottle on the shelf and took a sip of his drink. "Sorcerers imprisoned and tortured my friends and family. We suffered for a hundred years. I saw the information as dangerous, so I eliminated it." He took another sip of his drink, then set the glass down. While placing his hands on the bar, his eyes challenged Quinlin.

The dragon warlord was more ruthless than he had imagined, which made him very dangerous.

Quinlin took a deep breath and turned to Keren. "You're a sorcerer. How could you let him destroy the elders' library?"

She raised her eyebrows and put a hand to her chest. "Me? Let him?" She pointed at Calypso. "No one keeps Calypso from doing exactly what he wants to do."

Quinlin glared at Calypso when he saw a smirk on the dragon's face.

Calypso raised his glass. "But when I give my word, I follow through." He took a sip, then set the glass on the bar. "After you reverse Jewel's curse," he touched the artifact hanging around his neck, "you get the Amplification Disk."

Quinlin nodded. "Then I'm ready to reverse the curse."

He walked to the table and pushed the books aside. He laid the papers out so he could see them all.

"Hold on," Keren said. "I have to call..."

Quinlin didn't wait for her to finish. *"Sosepum peledus umpelo."*

Keren fumbled with her phone. She said something to someone on the other end, but Quinlin wasn't listening. He focused on the curse.

"Sosepum peledus umpelo remuvien confestim."

Keren's voice sounded frantic. He chuckled to himself. Wherever Jewel was at, there would now be a very large and angry Chinese dragon.

"It's done," Quinlin said. He turned to Calypso and held out his hand. "Give me the Amplification Disk."

CHAPTER TWENTY

KEREN

"Ryota!" Keren shouted with a breathy voice as she tried to keep Quinlin from overhearing. "Put Sirena on the phone." The noise in the background sounded like a demolition team working.

"You did it!" Sirena panted into the phone. "But you should have given me some time to get Jewel outside." Her voice changed to a scolding tone. "You could have seriously injured her. She's disoriented from the shock. I have to go."

"Is she alright?" Keren asked.

But Sirena hung up.

Keren gripped the phone in her hand. Quinlin had always gotten the better of her. But she couldn't let him know he'd gotten under her skin. She took some deep breaths to calm her pounding heart. When she felt more under control, she turned around to face him.

Quinlin stood at the dining room table, sorting through her mom's notes. A chill ran down her spine. Suddenly, she didn't want Quinlin to have anything to do with her mom or her personal notes. She wished her mom were here helping instead of Quinlin, but they were too far down this path to turn back now.

"It worked. You've restored Jewel to her natural form," Keren said.

Quinlin turned to Calypso and held out his hand.

Without speaking, Calypso's hand gripped the Amplification Disk. He slowly removed the artifact from around his neck. With it clenched in his hand, he pursed his lips, hesitating.

Keren couldn't breathe. If Calypso changed his mind about giving Quinlin the artifact, she had little hope of saving Katrina.

With a grunt, Calypso put the artifact in Quinlin's hand. "I won't release you until you've reversed the twisted curse." His voice deepened. "And you'll tell us when you're ready and won't proceed until we give the approval."

Quinlin smirked as he placed the Amplification Disk around his neck. "Making new rules for our arrangement?"

"Yes," Calypso said.

Quinlin's smile faded as he glared at Calypso. "I'll agree, out of courtesy to Keren."

Calypso raised an eyebrow. "You'll agree because I've given you no other choice."

The suffocating tension in the room sent Keren's heart racing again. Should she tell Calypso how Jewel's transformation had destroyed his home? No, probably not the best timing.

"You have two days, sorcerer." Calypso spat out the last word as if it had left a bad taste in his mouth. "If you don't have results by then, I'll have the pleasure of killing you myself."

Quinlin's body tensed, but he remained silent.

Calypso turned and strode toward the door.

"I'll be right back," Keren said to Quinlin. She trotted after Calypso.

After Keren closed the door and they walked down the hallway, she asked, "Are you alright?"

Calypso rounded on her. "I just placed the most powerful artifact that a sorcerer could use against dragons in the hands of a sorcerer." He shook his head and ran his fingers through his hair. "I must be insane to have agreed to this plan."

"It will work," Keren said. "And thanks."

He put his hand on the wall and leaned on it. "For what?"

"For lying about *The Creation of Sorcerers*," Keren said.

He stood straight and turned to her. "I don't lie. If you listened closely, everything I said was true."

Keren frowned. "I don't understand."

"I did destroy the elders' library. I let Quinlin assume that's where you found the information about Jewel's curse. I also allowed you to make photocopies of the pages on my office copy machine before we came here."

Keren thought back to the conversation. "But you were talking about two different circumstances and making them seem like one."

"Whatever Quinlin assumed from my words is his problem." He sighed. "That is the most dangerous sorcerer I've ever encountered. This plan had better work."

"It will work," she said. "I'll go in and see how he's doing with the twisted curse research." She bit her lip. "Oh, and Jewel's transformation might have damaged your house."

"My house?" Calypso's face turned red. "If Quinlin caused any harm to my family, I'll kill him today."

Before Keren could say anything, Calypso rushed into the waiting elevator.

"Well, that didn't go very well," Keren muttered.

As she turned to walk back into the penthouse, her phone buzzed. It was Briggs.

"Briggs?" Keren asked.

"Keren, what have you done?" Briggs asked.

Keren winced at the tone of his voice. "What do you mean?"

"Quinlin escaped from prison. But I'm certain you know that already," he growled into the phone.

"He did?" Her fake surprised voice didn't sound convincing to her. "When?"

"This afternoon. They said he had accomplices. Several of them." Briggs paused and took a breath. "Are you saying you know nothing about this?"

Keren bit her lip. If she told Briggs, he'd have to either turn her in or give up his career. She couldn't let either of those things happen. Her heart broke as the lies spilled from her mouth. "No, tell me what happened."

"I can't release details, but we suspect shifters helped him. There was evidence of elemental magic." His voice sounded urgent. "Where are you?"

"I'm headed back to Calypso's house," she said.

"I'll meet you there," Briggs said.

"No!" Keren shouted. Crap. If Briggs saw Calypso's damaged house and Jewel, he would figure out she was involved with Quinlin's escape. "I'm close to the station. I can meet you there."

"Alright." Briggs huffed out a breath. "Maybe you can help find Quinlin."

Keren swallowed the lump in her throat. "Me?"

"You stopped him the first time." He let out a deep breath. "I'm so glad you're not responsible for his escape. I'm sorry I jumped to conclusions."

"Yeah." Keren rubbed the back of her neck as guilt flooded through her. "I'll see you soon."

"I'll see you," Briggs said, then he hung up.

Crap. Crap. Crap. Keren paced the hallway. She wanted to stay with Quinlin and help research the twisted curse. Now Briggs wanted her to join the inquisitors' search to find Quinlin.

She'd have a brief talk with Quinlin, then meet Briggs at the station.

CHAPTER TWENTY-ONE

BRIGGS

Briggs pocketed his phone and scrubbed a hand over his hair. At least Keren wasn't involved with Quinlin's escape.

"Commander Wilson?" an officer said as he trotted toward Briggs. "The chief wants to see you. She's in the main conference room."

Briggs held up a finger. "I'll be right there." He hurried to the reception area. "Excuse me."

"Yes?" a young, red-lipped receptionist asked.

"Keren Stewart is arriving soon. When she gets here, will you have someone escort her to the main conference room?"

"I will, Commander Wilson," the receptionist said.

"Thanks." Briggs made his way to the main conference room.

When he stepped inside, he saw Officer Smythe and two other officers reviewing a whiteboard they had set up. Next to them stood the chief of the Las Vegas inquisitors. The wrinkles in her uniform and her messy, off-center ponytail made Briggs assume she hadn't been home for a few days.

The smell of freshly brewed coffee filled the air, a sure sign the officers planned for another very long day. The hairs on Briggs's neck bristled when he looked at the picture of Quinlin posted at the top of the board.

Briggs walked over to the group. "Chief, I've contacted Keren. She knows nothing about Turner's escape. I've asked her to come to the station."

Worry lines etched themselves into the chief's face. "There have been interesting developments." She turned to Smythe. "Tell Commander Wilson what you just told me."

Officer Smythe turned to face Briggs. "There have been five more murders of shifters. All the deaths are because of a dart gun with some type of liquid that drains shifter magic."

The chief interrupted. "Quinlin Turner wanted to eliminate the shifter races. Now he's free. We can't help but think there's a connection between these two incidents."

Briggs nodded. "I agree. Do you have evidence of any Dark Guild activity in Las Vegas?"

"None so far." The chief took a deep breath. "I'm going to be straight with you, Commander. I think Keren's involved."

Briggs winced. "She was never a member of the Dark Guild."

The chief eyed him. "I'm not saying she was or wasn't. What we know is Keren's a sorcerer, Quinlin Turner is on the loose, and shifters are dying. I'm willing to bet wherever she's at, so is he."

Briggs frowned. "She's responsible for putting Turner behind bars. Do you really think Keren is part of this?"

"I do," the chief said. "Ever since Keren arrived in Las Vegas, it's been one disaster after another. You can't deny that."

"But she saved the city from the dragons." Briggs's head spun. He couldn't believe what he was hearing.

"I know she's your friend, Commander. But step back and look at the facts. Everything circles back to her."

Briggs felt his heart pounding in his chest. "Are you planning to arrest her?"

"I don't have evidence yet. But when she gets here, I'll keep her for questioning." The chief raised an eyebrow. "I'm hoping to get information on the Dark Guild that will help us put an end to this slaughter. Once she sees what's happening, she might find sympathy for the shifters."

"She's not responsible!" Briggs shouted.

The room spun. How could the chief think Keren was involved?

"We'll see." The chief rubbed the back of her neck. "I have a great deal of respect for your work, Commander Wilson, but I feel your choice of friends is questionable."

When Briggs reached for his phone, the chief held out her hand. "Don't. We need her here."

He had to get word to Keren. She couldn't come down to the station.

CHAPTER TWENTY-TWO

QUINLIN

Quinlin secured his earpiece and walked out of the master bedroom to find Keren standing at the dining room table. He felt much better after scrubbing the slimy scum of the prison off his skin. Before prison, he would never have considered wearing the loose-fitting gray sweat pants and blue T-shirt Calypso had left for him. But today, they felt like the most luxurious clothes he'd ever worn.

Quinlin breathed a sigh of relief at seeing Keren and not Calypso. He'd hoped he'd seen the last of the dragon warlord.

Quinlin smiled at her. "I'm glad you joined me. I could use the help to sort through your mother's notes."

Keren hesitated, then walked over. She seemed distracted.

"Anything wrong?" Quinlin asked.

She shook her head. "No, just tired."

"That's understandable." He turned to face her and leaned on the table. "You've grown stronger since the last time I saw you."

"Have I?" she asked, still not fully in the conversation.

"You're distracted. Maybe you should take care of whatever is on your mind. I'll be fine here."

She shook her head. "No, really." Keren's eyes finally focused on him. "I want to help."

Quinlin smiled. "I'm glad." He raised an eyebrow. "We make a good team, you know."

She scrunched her nose, then walked to the table and picked up Marcus's grimoire. "Mom said the curse Marcus used was the third version of the conversion curse." Keren shuffled through the stack until she found her mother's notebook. "Mom also said she tagged the page where she wrote down as much of the twisted curse as she could remember after casting it." She flipped through the pages until she found the one that was tagged.

Quinlin took the notebook, letting his fingertips brush against hers. "This will speed things up." He looked up at her and gave another warm smile. "Thanks."

This time, she smiled back. Good. Her defenses were down.

He pretended to study the notebook. "Why do you want to get rid of your creatures? They're so powerful."

When she didn't answer right away, he looked up. Her face had paled.

"Are you being forced to get rid of them?" Quinlin asked. "If you are, I can protect you from whomever is threatening you."

She shook her head. "It's not that. I want them gone. They've been nothing but trouble from the start."

"I thought you were friends with your creatures." Quinlin put a hand on her shoulder, and she didn't pull away. "Everything you have is what my father dreamed of. What I swore to make a reality in his honor."

Terror filled her eyes as she stepped away. "You don't want this." She wiped a tear from her face. "I want a normal life."

Quinlin held back a sneer. Losers have normal lives. Followers with no ambition or dreams. "You have so much potential." He reached for her again, but she stepped further back.

"Reverse the curse, Quinlin. Or Calypso will kill you."

Anger bubbled in Quinlin's chest. "Why do you follow that dirty shifter? You have more power than he does."

Keren's phone buzzed, and she turned to answer it. Quinlin strained to hear what she was saying, but she was talking in too low of a voice.

Keren turned to him. "I have to take this call. I'll be right back." She pointed at the table. "You need to get to work."

Keren walked across the room and out of the penthouse.

Quinlin turned to the table. With the sweep of an arm, he sent the papers and books flying onto the floor.

"I am not a puppet for someone to command!" he shouted.

He slammed both fists on the table, enjoying the pain that radiated up his arms. He was a king, and they had him trapped here like an animal. His eyes looked at the blacked-out windows.

"What if I blast my way out?" he asked aloud. "How many dragons could there be?"

He scowled. From the breakout, he guessed there were at least a dozen. He didn't know how strong they were, but he was certain a twelve against one fight would end badly for him. Especially if one of those dragons was Calypso.

He sighed and bent down to pick up his father's grimoire. "I'll use what I learn here, Father, to create new creatures. Creatures like Keren's."

He set the grimoire on the table and picked up Keren's mother's notebook. He opened it to the page with the twisted curse.

"She's missing some words," he mumbled as he flipped the page. "But with the grimoire, I should be able to fill in the blanks rather quickly."

Good. The sooner he was out of there, the better. He had Theodore waiting for him, along with his dedicated followers.

CHAPTER TWENTY-THREE

KEREN

After Keren rushed out of the penthouse, she gave a wave to Petrov, then strode down the hall. He would hear her anyway, but being away from him made her feel like her conversation was private.

"Slow down, Sirena." Keren rubbed the back of her neck. "What is Jewel doing?"

"She's preparing to take back sorcerer magic," Sirena said, her voice sounding panicked.

"She has to wait." If Jewel were to take back sorcerer magic before Quinlin reversed the twisted curse, Itorn would continue to use Katrina's blood to kill shifters. "Can't you talk some sense into her?"

"Yeah, right," Sirena said. "She's a Chinese dragon."

"I know, but," Keren rubbed her face, "tell her to wait until I get there. I'll talk to her."

"She's building up strength," Sirena said. "I'm not sure how long it will take. You'd better hurry."

"I'm on my way." Keren hung up with Sirena and dialed Gaines.

"PIB. How can I help you?" Gaines sounded distracted.

"Gaines, I need a ride right now. I'm at the Paris Las Vegas."

"Keren?"

"Yeah. It's an emergency."

Now Gaines sounded focused. "Copy that. I'll be there in two minutes. I'll meet you on the roof."

"Thanks." Keren hung up and ran to the stairwell.

She sprinted up the stairs and busted out the door onto the roof. In front of her, six dragons sat perched on the side of the building. The green dragon turned when Keren appeared. The sun danced off the dragon's scales, which were shimmering with sparkles of yellow and silver.

Gabriel changed into her human form and walked over to Keren. "Is there trouble with Quinlin?"

Keren shook her head. "No. It's Jewel. She won't wait for Quinlin to reverse the curse before taking sorcerer magic."

A black dragon circled overhead, then landed on the roof. Gaines turned his back to Keren so she could climb on.

Both Keren and Gabriel ran toward Gaines.

"I have to talk to Jewel," Keren said as she scrambled onto Gaines's back. She pushed her hands under his scales to hang on. "Take me to Calypso's."

"I'll come with you," Gabriel said.

"OK, but I have to warn you. The curse's reversal damaged your house."

Gabriel frowned, but said nothing.

Gaines took off as Gabriel changed back into her dragon form. They both flew at top speed to Calypso's.

Keren gaped as Gaines approached Calypso's house. A large serpentlike creature stood where Calypso's drawing room used to be. Jewel's golden scales shimmered in the light. Two lines ran down her back. One was red spikes that reminded Keren of shark fins. The other was blue and looked more like hair as it flowed in the breeze. One long whisker protruded from each side of her face. She stood on two back feet while bracing her front feet on the house. Each foot had four sharp talons in the front and one in the back.

When they landed on the lawn, they noticed Gabriel was half the size of Jewel. Keren hopped off Gaines, and he transformed to his human form. He pressed his horse ears back against his head.

"What is that?" Gaines asked.

"That's Jewel," Keren said. She craned her neck to look up at Jewel's face. Running forward and waving her arms, Keren shouted, "Jewel, I want to talk to you."

A golden tail swished from inside the house. Rubble flew everywhere as the tail continued toward Keren.

"Look out!" Gaines shouted. But it was too late.

Jewel's tail hit Keren square in the chest. She flew backward and landed with a thud on the ground. The world blurred in and out of focus as Keren tried to stand up.

Gaines was at her side, pulling on her arm. "Come on, we have to get away."

She let him pull her to her feet. They both dove to the side as Jewel's tail came across the lawn for another blow.

"I have to talk to her," Keren said as she stumbled forward.

Gaines pulled on her arm. "No way. She'll kill you. You're a sorcerer."

"I have to try." Keren pulled her arm free and moved toward Jewel.

Gabriel took flight and circled over Jewel. Jewel looked up and roared at Gabriel. Then Gabriel perched on the side of the house in front of Jewel.

"What's she doing?" Gaines asked. "Jewel could crush her with one chomp."

Gabriel chirped and barked, and Jewel responded with similar noises.

"I think they're talking," Keren said. "Not telepathically."

Gabriel lowered her head, exposing the crest to Jewel. Jewel lowered her head and pressed her forehead against Gabriel and let out a long purr sound.

Keren searched for the pulse. She let the steady beat pound in her solar plexus, then it shot up her neck to the back of her eyes. Golden light exploded around her.

"One!" Keren shouted.

A mist formed over Keren's head, then One appeared. It did a somersault, then hovered in the air. She might not be able to telepathically talk to Jewel, but she could talk to Gabriel.

Gabriel, what's going on?

Jewel's frightened. The world has changed.

Can you talk to her?

In a sense. We share feelings. It's not words as you know them.

Can you ask her to wait to take sorcerer magic? I need to give Quinlin time to reverse the twisted curse.

I'll try.

Keren waited for several minutes as the two dragons barked and hissed at one another.

I'm sorry, said Gabriel. *She will not wait. She's afraid of being imprisoned again. Once she has enough strength, she will take the sorcerers' magic.*

Panic flowed like ice through Keren's veins. This was her only hope of saving Katrina.

How long will it take?

A day, maybe more, maybe less.

That wasn't much help.

She senses you're a sorcerer. She says it's wrong for you to wield elemental magic.

Tell her I agree. I'm trying to fix it. But she has to wait to take sorcerer magic.

She doesn't trust you. You must leave, or she will kill you.

The golden tail swung again in Keren's direction. One swooped down and picked her up just as the tail sailed underneath of them.

"One, take me back to the penthouse."

I'm going to hurry Quinlin along. Can you let me know when Jewel has her power back?

Yes, but I have no control over it or when she uses it, said Gabriel.

I understand.

Keren shouted down at Gaines. "Can your agents keep this area clear? We don't need anything spooking Jewel."

"I'm on it." Gaines pulled out his phone and typed out a message. He looked up at Keren. "Do you need a lift back to the penthouse?"

"No, thanks. I'll have One take me over." She shifted in One's grasp. "I have to get Quinlin to hurry."

"Good luck," Gaines said. He waved at Keren as One flew up then darted in the penthouse's direction. Crap, she'd completely forgotten about meeting Briggs at the station. She wiggled her hand into her pocket and pulled out her phone.

"Sorry," she typed. "Something came up and I'll be late getting to the station. I'll text when I'm on my way." She hit the send button and set her phone to silence. After pushing the phone back into her pocket, guilt gnawed at her heart. She should tell Briggs the truth, but she had to protect him and his career.

After One set her on the resort's roof, Keren released her magic, ran inside, then raced down one flight of stairs to the penthouse floor. She paused outside of the door to catch her breath, not wanting to let on to Quinlin that anything was wrong. He was too clever and attentive to not notice her agitation.

Giving herself a few minutes of privacy to compose herself, she went down one more flight of stairs. She clenched and unclenched her fists, and she paced the hall, taking deep breaths. When she walked by a mirror, she stopped and gasped. She looked terrible. Running her fingers through her hair, she did the best she could to smooth the tangled mess. Flying by dragon, and Jewel's attack, had made shambles of her clothes too.

She wiped dirt smudges from her forehead and practiced smiling. No, that one looked frightening. She tried again. Yikes, not that one. Way, way too guilty. She settled on a less toothy half grin. She took a deep breath in, then let it out slowly. She was ready to face Quinlin.

After taking the elevator up to the penthouse, she walked calmly to the door. She pushed it open and stepped inside.

Quinlin sat on the plush leather couch with his feet propped up on the coffee table. He had Marcus's grimoire open in his lap while he read her mom's notebook.

Without looking away from the notebook, he said, "You were gone for a while." He closed the notebook and glared at her. "Where did you go?"

Keren hadn't thought of an excuse before she came in, and her mind raced to find one now. "Calypso needed something."

He set the notebook aside and put his feet on the floor. Placing his elbows on his knees, he leaned forward. "You work for Calypso?"

"Yes," she answered quickly since, technically, it was true. At least according to the parole papers that Theodore had filed for her mom.

"What do you do?" Quinlin asked.

Theodore. His name flashed in her head like a warning beacon. He worked for Quinlin. She had to think of something believable. "Right now my job is to watch the Amplification Disk." She stepped into the room and sat in a chair across from Quinlin. "He was angry. It took time to calm him down. You do that to people, you know."

Quinlin smiled and leaned back on the couch. "I'm glad I got under the dragon's skin." He nodded to her. "And I'm glad to have you as my babysitter."

Keren cringed. She'd have to be careful of what she said around Quinlin. "Any luck with the twisted curse?"

"Actually," he picked up her mom's notebook, "your mother missed only a few details of the curse. I can piece together the rest."

"Good. When can you reverse it?" Keren shifted in the chair. Her mind wandered to Jewel.

Quinlin set the notebook aside. "You're that eager to throw away your gift?"

"It's not a gift, Quinlin. I told you, it's a curse. I've done nothing but hurt my friends and wreak havoc in the world. I need to get rid of it forever."

He scooted to the edge of his seat. "I could help you. You've surrounded yourself with people who've filled your mind with lies. Together, we could rule magic."

Keren sprang up. "There is no *we*, Quinlin. There never was."

"Never?" He lifted his eyebrows. "We had moments of intimacy."

Embarrassed, Keren couldn't stop herself from blushing. Heat prickled on her cheeks. "You fooled me once. Never again."

"Am I that repulsive to you?" Quinlin held out his hand. "Come sit next to me."

Keren shook her head. "No. Once the twisted curse is reversed, I hope to never see you again."

Quinlin held out his hand for a moment longer, then sighed. "The offer remains on the table. We'd be an unstoppable force."

"How many times do I have to say this? I don't want to be unstoppable. I want to be normal." Keren walked over to the dining room table. She noticed the pages from *The Creation of Sorcerers* were gone. Her heart skipped a beat. Why would Quinlin want those papers? She turned to face him. "Are you ready to reverse the twisted curse?"

Quinlin stood. "I am. Are you ready? I don't know what this will do to you."

A chill ran down Keren's spine.

"It could kill you."

When Keren didn't respond, Quinlin folded his arms. "You're being selfish, you know."

"Selfish?" Keren asked.

"Yes, my father and I worked for years to attain what you so carelessly want to throw away."

Keren looked at her mom's notebook clutched in Quinlin's hands. Panic raced through her as she realized he planned to use the twisted curse to steal elemental magic.

She held out her hand. "Give me Mom's notebook."

"No," Quinlin said.

"It's not yours." She stepped toward Quinlin, extending her hand further. "Give it to me. Briggs has to return it to Orlando."

"No. Your mother's notes complete the puzzle to sorcerers ruling elemental magic."

Keren felt the floor drop out from under her. She'd given Quinlin the tools to make another army. This one would be even more deadly.

"I won't let you keep it," Keren said.

"Once I reverse your twisted curse," Quinlin smiled, "you won't be able to stop me."

"Calypso can stop you." Keren's heart raced. She'd done it again. In her rush to save Katrina, she hadn't thought about what else Quinlin might do with the information.

Quinlin smiled. "You think you're so clever? My army is on its way here as we speak. I know I'm in Las Vegas at the Bellagio Hotel." He laughed. "The circling dragons gave away my location."

Keren's eyes bulged as she looked at the windows. They were still blacked out. How could he know about the dragons?

Quinlin tapped his ear. "Theodore sent me a going away present in prison." He smiled. "You can't outsmart me, Keren."

He grasped the Amplification Disk around his neck. "This artifact will strengthen my creatures. They'll be stronger than yours. It will also help me put the dragons in prison where they belong."

Keren's heart pounded in her chest. She felt for her phone, but hesitated. If Quinlin ran now, Katrina would spend the rest of her life as a blood slave to Itorn.

Tears streamed down her face. Tears out of fear for her sister. "Reverse the twisted curse. Take what you want. I just want to be done with all of this."

He sneered at her. "You're pitiful." He held out his palm toward her. "You don't deserve the honor of elemental magic."

Pain tore through Keren's chest. She fell to her knees, gasping for air. She couldn't hear what Quinlin was saying, but she knew he was chanting. She threw her head back and screamed as an invisible claw gutted her.

Then she felt warm breath on her ear.

"I could have made this less painful, but you deserve to be punished."

Quinlin started chanting again. It felt as though her limbs were being torn from her body. She screamed again as her body convulsed with pain. She had no control over her movements. She fell over, and her body jerked and twitched as the curse tore her to pieces.

One's picture flashed in her mind. It struggled to keep its wings open. Pieces of it disappeared. First one wing, then the other. Terror flooded through her. Her creatures were feeling the same pain. Mist swirled in her mind, then Two appeared. The wolf-bodied creature fought to stand. But when its horns turned to mist and disappeared, it fell to the ground in a heap. Finally, she saw Three. It thrashed from side to side holding both sides of its head. First, its head turned to mist and disappeared. Then its body fell lifeless to the ground and faded away.

Keren screamed again. What was Katrina feeling? Was the reversal spell even working on her?

CHAPTER TWENTY-FOUR

QUINLIN

Quinlin stood over Keren. Her convulsions had given her clawed hands, and she'd passed out from the pain.

"You should have joined me," he said. "Now, you're nothing."

He pulled the burner phone from his pocket and dialed the one number available.

"It's done," he said without waiting for whomever answered to say something. "Let me out of this prison."

"We need proof," the voice said on the other end. "Calypso will be there shortly."

Quinlin threw the phone across the room. He'd done his part. They'd never said Keren had to live through the experience.

He stooped down and felt for a pulse. It was weak, but there. He pulled her to a sitting position and dragged her to the couch. After heaving her onto it, he set her arms and legs in normal positions. Then he went to the kitchen for some ice.

He heard the penthouse door open and close. That must be Calypso. Quinlin pulled a steak knife from the block on the counter and slid it into his waistband. He covered it with his shirt. After twisting a kitchen towel around some ice, he walked into the living room.

He saw Calypso standing over Keren. Quinlin tried to decipher the look on the dragon's face, but he showed no emotion.

"It was rough on her," Quinlin said in the most caring voice he could muster. He stepped forward and extended the towel. "Here's some ice. It might help revive her."

Quinlin snarled when Calypso stepped back and put his hands behind his back. Quinlin walked to the couch and held the ice to Keren's forehead.

"I've done my part," Quinlin said. "Let me go."

"Once I've confirmed it worked." Calypso put his hands behind his back and moved around the couch, never taking his eyes off Quinlin.

Quinlin sighed and reached down to shake Keren's shoulder. At first, he gave her a gentle shake, then one more forceful.

He looked at Calypso. "She's out cold."

Calypso raised one eyebrow but said nothing.

Quinlin huffed and set the ice on the coffee table. He shook Keren and slapped her cheek. "Keren, wake up." He shook her again. "Keren," he said in a sterner tone.

Hope sparked in Quinlin chest when she made a noise. He reached back for the ice and pressed it to her forehead. "That's right. Time to wake up."

Keren's eyes fluttered open. Suddenly, pain rushed through Quinlin's jaw as Keren's right hook slammed into his face. He stumbled back and bumped into the coffee table. Thrown off-balance, he crashed back onto the table, jamming his elbow into the glass, causing it to shatter beneath him.

CHAPTER TWENTY-FIVE

KEREN

Keren tried to point a finger at Quinlin, but her arm moved uncontrollably, like jelly. "You tortured them," she croaked. Her throat burned from the effort.

She felt the couch sag next to her and a warm hand on her shoulder.

"Keren," Calypso grabbed her chin and turned her head toward his face, "did the reversal work?"

She tried to focus on Calypso. "He tortured them. He tore them apart piece by piece."

She heard Quinlin's sharp tone. "The creatures were bound by the twisted curse. Of course the reversal would tear them apart."

A tear dripped down her face. What had she expected?

"You didn't have to," she forced out.

She felt hands on either side of her face. Calypso stared into her eyes. She tried to focus on his face, but he kept blurring out of focus.

"Did it work?" the dragon warlord asked.

More tears dripped down her cheeks. "I don't know."

"Try to summon your magic," Quinlin said.

Calypso lowered her head onto the back of the couch. "She's too weak. I'll take her to where she can recover."

"You said you'd keep your word and set me free once my part was done," Quinlin said.

She felt Calypso leave the couch. "I will, once I've confirmed you've completed your end of the bargain."

Quinlin laughed. The sound sent a chill through Keren's body.

"My army is on its way here. You can't keep me prisoner."

"Your army is in Las Vegas, searching the Bellagio Hotel as we speak." Calypso chuckled. "But they won't find you."

Quinlin's face grew dark. "What do you mean?"

Keren laughed. The movement was painful, but she didn't care. She lifted her head to look at Quinlin. "You're not at the Bellagio."

Quinlin let out a guttural yell as he pulled a knife from his waistband. He raised it over his head and lunged at Keren. Horror and panic raced through her. She wanted to move, but couldn't. As fast as lightning, Calypso had a hand on Quinlin's wrist.

"I should kill you," the dragon warlord growled.

Calypso took the knife from Quinlin's hand and tucked it into his belt. Then he pushed Quinlin aside.

Keren's eyes drifted shut. She felt her body lift from the couch. Heat radiated from Calypso as she fell onto his chest. She closed her eyes and snuggled close to him. His voice vibrated in his chest.

"I'll release you after I've confirmed the curse's reversal," Calypso said.

She heard the bang of a door, then another. She opened her eyes and realized they were in the stairwell.

"Where are we going? Stop Quinlin." Her voice faded as she ran out of strength to talk.

"I'm taking you to a hospital," Calypso said.

"No, take me to Jewel. Quinlin ..." Keren coughed. "Quinlin has to be stopped."

Calypso paused. "What are you talking about?"

Keren forced a deep breath into her lungs. "He's planning to use the twisted curse to create another army and annihilate shifters."

"He'll never get the chance." Calypso's deep growl radiated through Keren's body.

She felt a cool breeze on her face. They must be on the roof. Then she felt the cold concrete against her skin as Calypso set her down. Moments later, rough talons wrapped around her. Her stomach lurched as Calypso took to the sky.

She forced herself to search for the pulse. Every inch of her body ached as she became more frantic searching for it. Just one more time, she thought. She had to make sure her creatures were alright.

Tears streamed down her face when the only beat she found was her racing heart. Quinlin had done it. He'd reversed the twisted curse.

She felt hollow. Quinlin had torn a part of her away. Her creatures had been with her since the age of three. Had she made the right decision?

CHAPTER TWENTY-SIX

BRIGGS

Briggs jumped as Jordon burst in to the conference room. Sweat beaded on Jordon's furrowed brow. "Sorcerers are attacking the Bellagio."

"Sorcerers?" the chief asked. "Are you certain?"

"Yes." Jordon rushed to Briggs and grabbed his arm. "We have to go."

The chief held out her hand. "Briggs isn't going anywhere. We're waiting for Keren."

"She's not coming," Briggs said as he waved his phone in the air. "She messaged me a few minutes ago." He hoped the chief didn't want to read the message.

The chief put her hands on her hips. "Come clean, Wilson. Is Keren part of the sorcerers' attack?"

"How do I know?" Briggs yelled. "If you let me go, I'll find out."

"Briggs," Jordon interrupted. "The PIB reported seeing Keren."

Anger flared on the chief's face. "Find her, Commander Wilson, and bring her back here."

Not taking the time to acknowledge the chief's order, Briggs bolted from the conference room. Jordon followed close behind.

Briggs hopped into a police car, and Jordon joined him in the passenger's seat. The car's tires screeched as Briggs pulled out of the parking lot and headed toward the Bellagio. "Is Turner with them?"

Jordon shook his head. "No one has mentioned seeing Turner."

The look on Jordon's face worried Briggs.

"What aren't you telling me?" Briggs asked.

"Gaines sent me to find you. He told me the sorcerers are looking for Turner." Jordon turned to face Briggs. "Commander, if Turner isn't with the sorcerers, then who broke him out of jail?"

Dread rumbled in the pit of Briggs's stomach. He could only think of one explanation. But if Keren was with the sorcerers, that meant she was also looking for Turner. It made little sense.

Briggs slammed on the brakes next to a van with *PIB* painted on the side in large white letters. He saw Gaines standing outside the van. Across the street stood the Bellagio. Sorcerers' energy blasts lit up the sky. A dozen dragons circled over the resort, raining fire down onto the sorcerers.

"Gaines," Briggs said as he trotted over with Jordon right behind him, "give me an update."

"Sorcerers are attacking the Bellagio." Gaines pointed to the sides of the resort. "Two inquisitor squads are in position on either side of the resort, but they aren't moving in. So far, the sorcerers are focusing on getting inside the building and shooting at the dragons."

Gaines pointed at the dragons. "Look, the dragons seem to be just taunting the sorcerers. They aren't interested in an all-out battle. If you look closely at the sorcerers on the roof, you'll see they're using dart guns against the dragons. Of course, the darts can't penetrate the dragons' scales."

"So, it was the sorcerers who killed those two inquisitor squads," Briggs growled. "I feel like I'm reliving a nightmare."

"Look." Jordon motioned down the street. "More inquisitors are showing up. I'm going to warn them about the darts."

Briggs saw at least six police cars racing down the strip. Shifters had no defense against darts tainted with Katrina's blood. He patted Jordon on the back. "Good idea. Stay down."

"Yes, Commander," Jordon said. Then he ran down the street toward the oncoming cars.

Briggs turned back to Gaines. "You saw Keren with the sorcerers?"

Gaines shook his head. "No me. Two agents reported seeing her."

Briggs's heart sank. He tried to puzzle out why she'd be with the sorcerers. Every idea he had ended up including Quinlin Turner.

Gaines put a hand on his arm. "Briggs."

Briggs snapped back to the moment. "Yeah, I'm fine."

Gaines lowered his voice. "I don't think it's Keren. The woman the agents identified is with Itorn."

"Katrina." The name came out of Briggs's mouth in a whisper. He pulled out his phone and texted Keren, "Where are you?"

"Come on," Briggs said as he stared at his phone. After a few minutes, he huffed and stuffed his phone back into his pocket. "She's not answering."

Briggs ducked as an explosion rang out behind him. He spun around and gaped at the large hole that had been blasted into the side of the top floor of the Paris Las Vegas resort. Dragons seemed to appear from out of nowhere. They circled around the opening, spewing fire into the resort.

"Holy hell, where did those dragons come from?" Gaines asked.

"They must have been on the roof." Briggs looked up as the dragons from the Bellagio zipped overhead. "They're headed to the Paris Las Vegas to join the other dragons."

Briggs and Gaines flattened themselves against the PIB truck as streams of fire lashed out at the Paris Las Vegas.

An energy blast flew from the resort. It clipped an orange dragon's wing, injuring it but not keeping it from flight. Another blast, and then another, shot from the resort.

"Briggs!" Gaines shouted as he pulled on Briggs's arm.

Briggs spun again. Sorcerers were streaming out of the Bellagio. There must have been sixty of them, and more were still flowing from the resort. Several carried dart rifles. They headed directly toward the Paris Las Vegas. The PIB van, Gaines, and Briggs stood directly in their path.

Gaines pointed at a crow flying over the hoard of sorcerers heading their way. "Look."

Briggs squinted. "An agent?"

"Yes. Look below her."

Briggs squinted at the crowd running under the crow. He caught his breath. There was Itorn, pulling Katrina behind him.

CHAPTER TWENTY-SEVEN

KEREN

After Calypso set Keren down, she struggled to get to her feet. Her stomach churned. She turned to the side and threw up whatever meager food remained in her stomach.

Keren wiped her mouth with her sleeve, then stood tall. She could do this. She had to stop Quinlin.

She looked at Calypso's demolished house. The gaping hole looked like the maw of a giant monster with teeth of hanging shingles. Jewel had settled onto the lawn. The red spikes on her back pulsed with light. Gabriel sat close to Jewel with her neck draped over the Chinese dragon's foot. Calypso landed next to his mate. He shuffled nervously before settling down and draping his large red wing over Gabriel.

Keren reached for her pulse. She had to find out how far Jewel's power had come. She shivered. Her insides were desolate, like a desert with tumbleweeds.

She took a deep breath. There was no turning back now. Each footstep plodded forward as she willed herself to move toward Jewel. From next to Jewel, Keren saw a hand wave in the air. The slender figure ran toward her.

"Keren!" Sirena shouted. "You shouldn't be here. You'll upset Jewel."

She skidded to a stop a few feet from Keren. "Oh my gosh. What happened to you?" The mermaid rushed over and wrapped her arms around Keren. "Sit down."

Keren couldn't muster the strength to hug her back. "No, I have to talk to Jewel."

"That's not a good idea," Sirena said. "She attacked you the last time you were here. She's much stronger now."

"I have to." Keren pushed Sirena aside and continued toward Jewel. "Jewel!" Keren shouted.

Jewel raised her head. Deep-blue eyes met Keren's stare. Smoke puffed out of Jewel's nostrils and the whiskers on the sides of her face twitched. In three strides, the Chinese dragon stood over Keren.

Keren watched Jewel's front talon pull back, then aim directly at her.

"Keren!" Sirena screamed.

The painful blow threw Keren across the driveway. She landed on the lawn, rolling several times before coming to a stop. Taking a deep breath, she let the earthy smell soak into her lungs. Thoughts of Briggs flashed in her mind. Saving shifters and her sister was all that mattered now. She wondered if she'd ever see Briggs again.

She pushed herself up from the ground. A painful gash across her left arm dripped blood.

"When will you be ready to take sorcerers' magic?" Keren asked as she stumbled toward Jewel.

Sirena ran to Keren. "Keren, stop. This isn't a good idea." The mermaid tried to push Keren aside, but Keren stood her ground.

"I no longer have elemental magic," Keren shouted at Jewel. "I want you to take away my sorcerer magic."

Jewel's whiskers fluttered. With one step, she was next to Keren again. Jewel lowered her head so one large blue eye stared at Keren.

"Jewel says you're telling the truth," Sirena said. "So, Quinlin reversed the twisted curse?"

"Yes," Keren said. "Now he has the Amplification Disk and the information to imbue more humans with elemental magic. Jewel, please, you have to stop him before he eliminates all shifters."

Jewel blinked, and a puff of smoke came from her nostrils.

"What about Katrina?" Sirena asked.

Keren wiped tears from her eyes. She had no time for sorrow. When this was over, if she was still alive, she'd find Katrina. If she died, she hoped Briggs would take care of her sister.

"I don't know. We need sorcerer magic to end. How close is Jewel from full power?"

"I'll ask." Sirena scrunched her nose, concentrating on Jewel. She shook her head. "Jewel's not sure. She'll know when she gets there."

Keren wiped a hand over her forehead. Jewel might be too late to stop Quinlin.

CHAPTER
TWENTY-EIGHT

BRIGGS

"I have to save Katrina," Briggs said.

"No." Gaines pulled Briggs down behind the PIB van. "You'll get darted as soon as they see you coming."

"You said a dragon's scales are too strong for the darts to penetrate." Briggs put his hand on Gaines's shoulder. "You can protect me."

Gaines shook his head. "I'm one dragon. There are at least twenty or more sorcerers with rifles."

"The agent watching Katrina," Briggs squeezed Gaines shoulder, "she can help." Briggs lowered his head and took a deep breath. When he looked up, he stared into Gaines's eyes. "I have to do this. For Keren."

While rubbing the back of his neck, Gaines shook his head. "This is suicide."

Briggs pursed his lips while keeping his eyes glued on Gaines's. His heart raced. This was his chance to save Keren's sister.

"Fine," Gaines huffed. "It's your funeral. Take cover under the van until I give you the signal that Itorn's close."

"What's the signal?" Briggs asked.

Gaines smiled and stepped away from the PIB van. "You can't miss it." The puca's neck lengthened, and he hunched over as black wings sprouted from his back. Now in his full dragon form, Gaines roared and sprung into the air.

Briggs dropped to the ground and marine crawled under the PIB van. He peered out as hundreds of feet stampeded in his direction.

Then the hoard of sorcerers overtook the PIB van. The vehicle rocked as sorcerers maneuvered their way around or over the top. A sorcerer tripped and fell onto the ground on his side, directly facing Briggs.

Their eyes met, then the sorcerer sneered and shouted, "Shifter!"

Briggs shot his hand out and grabbed onto the sorcerer's shirt front. He yanked the sorcerer under the van with him. The sorcerer flailed and kicked as he continued to shout. Pain shot through Briggs's knee, and a fist smashed into his chin.

Between the struggling sorcerer and Briggs's wide shoulders, Briggs had little room to move. Since the tight space had his other arm pinned underneath him, Briggs jerked the sorcerer closer, headbutting him to keep him quiet.

Briggs shook his head to clear his vision after the impact. The blow had dazed the sorcerer. His mouth hung open, and his eyes were closed.

"Sorry," Briggs muttered. He'd just wanted him to stop shouting. He took the sorcerer's pulse to confirm he was alive.

Thundering footfalls and cries of an angry mob raged past them. No one seemed to notice, or care, that the sorcerer had disappeared from their ranks.

Briggs pressed the hand of his pinned arm to the ground. Vines snaked up from the ground and wrapped themselves around the sorcerer. They secured the sorcerer's mouth, legs, and hands, then they dragged him away from Briggs.

His eyes darted around. The crowd had thinned. Most of the sorcerers had passed by already. A drop of sweat dripped into Briggs's eye, and he wiped his hand across his face and forehead. Feeling warmth, Briggs held his hand in front of him. Blood stained his palm. He glanced down at the unconscious sorcerer.

"I'll send medics," Briggs said to him.

Worried the struggle with the sorcerer had caused him to miss Gaines's signal, Briggs prepared to take action. When he moved, a sharp pain detonated in his knee like an explosion. He gritted his teeth, holding in a yell. Not able to marine crawl out from under the van, Briggs positioned himself longways near the edge. He planned to roll out and use the van to help get himself to his feet.

As he settled near the edge, he looked out at the few remaining sets of feet running toward him. He could take those sorcerers, he told himself. After a deep breath, he rolled out from under the van.

Just as he began rolling, a black ball rumbled by him. He heard screams and yells from the sorcerers. A black dragon landed between him and the oncoming people. Briggs looked up to where the ball had rolled. It unfurled into Gaines. He'd mowed down an entire line of sorcerers like they were bowling pins.

"I need help to stand," Briggs said to the agent in front of him. The agent shifted her tail closer to Briggs. He hauled himself up. After trying to put weight on his leg with the wounded knee, he winced and hissed in a breath. His leg was useless.

Gaines roared.

Briggs heard Itorn's voice. "Get away from me, puca, before I blast you to pieces."

"Let me through." Briggs pushed on the agent's tail. The black dragon shuffled to the side, revealing Itorn.

Itorn wore his ceremonial elder robes. The beige robes draped loosely around his body. A yellow cord served as a belt. Several bags of what Briggs thought must be potions or magic artifacts hung from the cord. Falling over one shoulder was a sash that had a bronze leaflike clip secured over the opposite hip. Over the other shoulder was a dart rifle.

Behind him, two similarly dressed sorcerers held Katrina. She wore white robes that made her already slim frame look emaciated. Her head fell forward and her hair hung down over her face.

Itorn's lip curled into a snarl. "Briggs."

Briggs stood as tall as he could while balancing on one foot. "Itorn, let Katrina go."

The elder sorcerer's head fell back as he bellowed a laugh. Then his deranged gaze fell on Briggs. "You can't tell me what to do." He pointed a finger at Briggs. "Your dirty shifters' time is over in this world. It's our time now." His eyes flit to the side.

Briggs fell to the ground as an energy blast sailed over. The blast struck the agent in the side. She roared in pain, then staggered away.

"No!" Briggs shouted.

The agent transformed into her human form before collapsing to the ground.

Briggs slammed his hand to the concrete. Vines and branches erupted from the ground, creating a domed cover over the agent. Another energy blast struck the dome. It nearly got through. Briggs quickly repaired the dome.

"Gaines!" Briggs shouted. "Get the agent to safety."

"Always the hero," Itorn said as he strode casually to the side. "I'll tell you what. I'm feeling generous today. I'll let the pucas go, but you're mine."

Briggs looked at Itorn's face. His eyes were blazing with hatred and anger. Where had that come from? Had he always been hiding such rage?

"Agreed," Briggs said. He opened the dome to Gaines as the dragon approached.

Gaines looked at Briggs.

"It's OK, Gaines. I'll be fine. Get her to a hospital."

The black dragon hesitated. After Briggs gave him another nod, Gaines picked up the agent in his talons and flew away.

"Get him to his feet," Itorn ordered.

One sorcerer came over and yanked Briggs up. Briggs pushed him away, but his injured leg caused him to lose his balance, and he fell to the ground. He twisted around, getting another look at Katrina's limp, withered body. Disgust for Itorn swirled in his gut.

"How much blood have you taken from her?" Briggs demanded.

"All that I've needed," Itorn said. He exaggeratingly puffed out his lower lip. "Oh, you're injured. Too bad. I'd hoped to kill you at your full strength. No matter." He nodded to the sorcerer, who hoisted Briggs up.

The sorcerer slammed Briggs against the PIB van and pushed his face close. "Now you'll get what you deserve." He gave Briggs a slight shove, then stepped aside.

Itorn took the rifle from his shoulder. "I hope you said your goodbyes to Keren." He cocked the chamber and aimed at Briggs.

"In cold blood? You've sunk to the lowest levels," Briggs said.

"I'm cleansing the earth," Itorn said as he pulled the trigger.

The dart landed square on Briggs's chest. The close range made it feel like a truck had slammed into him. He grunted and pitched forward but caught himself before he fell. So this was it. He took a deep breath, waiting for Katrina's blood to drain his magic, and his life, away. Thoughts of Keren in their earlier years flashed in his mind. He'd followed her around like a puppy dog throughout high school.

Keren's warmhearted laugh and kind nature had him entranced from the day he'd met her. Who was he kidding? She was drop-dead gorgeous.

Briggs glanced up. Itorn had a confused look on his face. By now all the other sorcerers had passed, leaving only Itorn, the two holding Katrina, and the one who'd man-handled Briggs. Briggs looked back down at the ground. Nothing was happening. Other than the pulsing pain in his knee and bruised chest, he felt fine.

With a yell, Briggs toppled to the side. He allowed himself a brief glimpse of Itorn. The elder sorcerer had reshouldered his rifle and was sporting a smug smirk on his face.

Briggs laid it on thick. He moaned and writhed on the ground. In the final throws of his award-winning death scene, he rolled onto his back. With his last bloodcurdling wail, he slapped both his palms flat to the ground and he held his breath.

"I'll never tire of watching that," a sorcerer said.

"Yes, it's gratifying," Itorn said. "Let's hurry. They should have found Mr. Turner by now."

Briggs's heart pounded. All this time, the elders had been working with Marcus, Quinlin, and the Dark Guild. He clenched his teeth together as he pressed his fingertips into the ground. Four thick roots shot out of the ground like spears as Briggs let out a heart-wrenching howl.

Then silence filled the air. Briggs squeezed his eyes shut. A tear dripped down the side of his face. He'd let his rage get the better of him. He'd stooped to their level. Slowly, he rolled to his stomach and pushed up to his feet. He took a deep breath and opened his eyes.

He gasped at the gruesome sight. A root held each of the four sorcerers suspended from the ground. The roots had pierced through the sorcerers' mouths and were sticking out of the backs of their heads.

Briggs stepped up to Itorn's unmoving body. "Consider the earth cleansed." He spat on the ground beneath the elder sorcerer.

He heard a moan, and his head snapped over to Katrina, who lay on the ground between two dangling sorcerers. He hurried over to her.

"Katrina?" Briggs held a hand over her back. The dart could have been empty or defective. She moaned again. Briggs pursed his lips, then grabbed her shoulder and turned her over. He waited for the painful magic drain, but it never came. Keren had done it. She'd reversed the twisted curse.

He pushed Katrina's hair back from her forehead and ran his hand down her face. Her skin was burning up.

"I'll get help." Briggs tried to stand, but his knee gave out, and he fell back onto the ground.

CHAPTER
TWENTY-NINE

KEREN

Ryota rushed from the mansion, waving his arms in the air. He ran toward Calypso and shouted, "Sir, Quinlin has escaped!"

"No!" Keren shouted. She looked into Jewel's eye. "Please, take the sorcerers' magic before it's too late."

Calypso stepped away from Gabriel and shifted into his human form. He waved an arm at Ryota, motioning him to follow, and trotted toward Keren.

When they reached Keren, Calypso said, "Ryota, give me your report."

"Sir, Quinlin used an energy blast to blow out the side of the penthouse. Unfortunately, sorcerers were already raiding the Bellagio. The decoy dragons worked as planned. However, after the blast, they quickly surmised Quinlin was in the Paris Las Vegas. The dragons are battling the sorcerers as we speak."

"And Quinlin?" Keren asked. "Did you find him?" If Quinlin were free, he'd waste no time using the Amplification Disk and the twisted curse to steal elemental magic.

"No. Petrov is searching but hasn't located him yet." Ryota looked at Calypso. "What are your orders, sir?"

Gabriel stepped up behind Calypso. She lay down and slid her nose under his hand. A low purr rumbled in her throat.

Calypso gave her a gentle pat. "I'm staying with Gabriel and Jewel. Our best defense is having Jewel strip the sorcerers of their magic. Gabriel believes her presence has helped Jewel's recovery, but Gabriel tires. My presence here is our best chance of getting Jewel's strength up." He looked at Keren. "You'll go with Ryota to find Quinlin."

Keren shook her head. "I no longer have elemental magic."

With squinted eyes, Calypso studied Keren. "You're certain?"

She nodded. "Yes."

"You still have sorcerer magic. And you know Quinlin better than anyone. It's best if you go." He looked at Ryota. "Take the Amplification Disk from Quinlin, no matter what the cost."

Ryota nodded. "I understand, sir."

"Wait!" Sirena shouted. She ran over to Ryota. "The elves can help. My army is ready."

Ryota smiled at Sirena. "Your help is welcome."

Sirena smiled back. "I'll get General Zaim to organize the attack." Then she ran off toward the mansion.

"I'll fly you over," Ryota said to Keren. "The elven army is on foot. They will take a while to get organized for an attack."

"Alright," Keren said.

She followed Ryota away from Jewel. She felt sore and drained. Her sorcerer magic was amateur at best. Regardless, she'd fight with the dragons. She had to find Quinlin and stop him from annihilating shifters.

After Ryota shifted to his dragon form, she climbed onto his back. With Keren's hands clutching his neck, the dragon sprang into the air. Below, Keren saw Jewel, Gabriel, and Calypso, who was now in his dragon form, huddled together. The red spikes on Jewel's back continued to pulse with power.

"Hurry, Jewel," Keren said.

When Ryota banked, she no longer saw the mansion. With a roar, Ryota surged with speed toward the Paris Las Vegas resort.

Keren saw the battle long before they arrived. Dragons circled in the sky, raining fire down on the sorcerers below. Sorcerer energy blasts shot up from the ground. The dragons danced around the attacks with ease.

Neither side looked like it had an advantage. It could come down to who tired first.

As they approached, Ryota swooped close to the ground. His speed slowed as he tipped to the side.

"You want me to jump off?" Keren asked.

A rumble came from Ryota, and he tipped again.

Keren looked down at the ground racing by. Even at a slower speed, Ryota must have been flying at thirty miles per hour or more. She held her breath and launched herself off the dragon.

She grunted as she landed on her shoulder and rolled several times. For a moment, she lay on the ground, unable to move. Her bruised and battered body begged her to give up. She'd lived with her creatures for over twenty years. Now that they were gone, her body felt feeble and worn out.

Willing herself to sit up, she watched Ryota join the other dragons. His appearance and new energy brought a surge of life to the dragons' attack.

Keren forced herself to stand. Her injured arm hung limply from her side. The bleeding had stopped, but she'd lost feeling in the arm.

She raised her good arm, her palm facing the mob of sorcerers.

"*Postestantenum*," Keren said.

White light spun into an energy ball, and it flew toward the unexpecting crowd. Cries rang out as Keren's energy ball tore through a group of sorcerers. Several turned in her direction. They raised their palms and returned her attack.

Keren crouched. "*Protegioum*," she shouted.

A shield gleamed around her as three energy balls struck. She screamed as the force of the attack pushed her to her limits. The tips of her fingers blackened, and black specs dotted her forearm. She couldn't take many more hits like that.

As the second wave of energy balls surged toward her, she rolled to the side. The hair on her arms sizzled as the energy balls passed by. That was close, too close. Her eyes darted around, looking for cover. A few yards away sat a squad car. She sprinted, putting the squad car between herself and the approaching half dozen sorcerers.

Keren's shock at seeing an inquisitor in the driver's seat made her wonder why he wasn't helping to fight the sorcerers. Was he injured? She banged on the driver-side window. "Open up. Are you OK?"

The window moved halfway down, then stopped. A wolf shifter with dark brown eyes and bushy eyebrows frowned at her. "You need to step back from the car. Go back to your sorcerer group."

"What? They're not *my* sorcerer group. We have to stop them." Keren tried to reach in, but the wolf shifter blocked her arm.

"I said back away," the wolf shifter said as the squad car's engine roared to life.

"We're not going anywhere," a familiar voice said.

Keren looked at the passenger. Relief flooded through her when she recognized Jordon. "What's happening?" she asked.

Jordon reached for the keys and shut off the engine. "The chief ordered all inquisitors to stand down."

"Why?" Keren asked.

The wolf shifter snorted. "We know sorcerers have a potion that kills shifters. We're waiting to see who wins the war between the dragons and sorcerers. Either way, the fight will reduce their numbers." He held out his hand to Jordon. "Give me the keys."

Keren grabbed the window with her good hand. "You're sacrificing the dragons? They're shifters too. We have to join forces."

The wolf shifter sneered at Keren's blackened fingertips. "And you're a sorcerer. Go back with your kind."

"I'll fight," Jordon said as he opened his door.

The wolf shifter's head snapped to Jordon. "You're disobeying a direct order. They'll suspend you."

Jordon tore off his badge and tossed it into the car. "I quit." He dangled the keys in front of him. "We're keeping the squad car."

With a growl, the wolf shifter opened his door, almost knocking Keren off her feet. He raced across the street away from Keren.

Keren clung to the door to keep her balance. "Jordon! Behind you!"

Three sorcerers had dart rifles pointed at the ex-inquisitor.

Ping. Ping. Ping.

The three darts bounced off the squad car as Jordon crouched and scrambled to Keren's side. Then he turned and returned fire with a water jet.

He hit one sorcerer holding a rifle, directly in the face, knocking him backward. Like snapping a whip, Jordon jerked the water jet to strike the second rifle-bearing sorcerer, then the third.

Keren braced herself on the squad car and held her palm out.

"*Postestantenum!*" she shouted. The recoil of the blast sent Keren flying backward. She lay sprawled on the ground, her arm throbbing in pain.

Jordon pulled her to her feet. "Come on. The energy blast knocked the remaining three sorcerers down. But we need to take cover." Jordon looked around. Then he pointed behind them. "Back there. I see PIB vans."

Keren leaned on Jordon. She tried to keep up, but her legs kept giving out.

"Let me carry you." Jordon lifted her into his arms and started running across the road.

"Stop!"

The command brought Jordon to a standstill.

Keren cringed. She peeked over Jordon's shoulder and saw Quinlin standing behind them.

"You're surrounded. I have twenty sorcerers with me who are ready to either dart you or blow you to pieces."

Keren felt Jordon's heart racing. His breath came in long, heavy draws.

"We can go out fighting," he whispered to her.

"No," Keren said. "We can't outpower him. We have to outwit him."

Jordon gave a slight nod.

"Jordon?" Quinlin asked as he walked around to face them. "I see you've recovered. So good to see you again."

Jordon ground his teeth, but he stood still.

"Put Keren down and step away. Slowly."

As Keren's weight shifted to the ground, she used Jordon's shoulder to steady herself before letting him go. "Don't hurt him."

When Quinlin tilted his head, two sorcerers ran over and grabbed Jordon's arms. One held a dart inches from Jordon's neck.

"First, our inquisitor friend will watch me beat you to death."

Keren gasped as her throat tightened. Her eyes darted to Jordon, then back to Quinlin.

Quinlin shrugged. "It's payback, Keren. You made me look like a fool. You must die by my hand." He stepped up to her and brushed a strand of hair from her face. Her skin crawled at his touch. "We could have been unstoppable." His hand pulled back, then his palm landed full force on her cheek.

The blow sent Keren staggering backward, but she stayed standing.

"Stop it!" Jordon shouted.

Quinlin stomped up to Jordon and pushed a finger into his chest. "Every word from you will make her death that much more excruciating."

Jordon opened his mouth, then snapped it shut. His sympathetic eyes looked at Keren.

"It's OK, Jordon," Keren said. She rubbed the side of her face.

Quinlin turned to face her. "Yes, it is OK, Keren." He put his hands behind his back as he walked over. "I have the twisted curse." He touched the Amplification Disk. "And the artifact that will increase the curse's impact. I'd say everything is OK."

Keren looked up at Quinlin. "You won't win."

Quinlin frowned. "You have no creatures, Keren. I took them away, remember?" He smiled. "But then, how could you forget?"

Anger boiled inside her. She lunged for Quinlin and scratched her nails across his face. He yelled out in pain, then pushed her to the ground.

While holding a hand to his scratched cheek, he walked up to Keren and kicked her in the ribs.

Agonizing pain erupted through her body. He kicked her again and again. Keren crunched into a fetal position trying to protect herself. She turned a palm out.

"*Protegioum.*"

The shield created a barrier between her and Quinlin.

"What a pathetic show of power. You're a disgrace to sorcery." Quinlin spat on the ground.

He continued kicking the shield. With each strike, Keren felt a fire burning in her hand and arm.

"You!" Quinlin kicked the shield. "Will!" He kicked again. Spittle shot from his mouth. "Die!" The crazed look in Quinlin's eyes told Keren he'd finally fallen into the abyss of utter madness.

"Turner!" Briggs's voice boomed. "Put your hands up. You're under arrest."

Quinlin stopped his assault on Keren's shield. With a sigh of relief, she released the spell. Her burned arm fell limply to the ground.

"Briggs." Quinlin laughed. "You're too late to be the hero." He swept a hand in Keren's direction. "Keren's creatures are gone, and you're outnumbered." He used both hands to push back his hair. Then he brushed off and straightened his shirt. "It is fitting, though, that you get to see her die."

"You're going back to prison, Turner. Give up. It's over."

Quinlin pressed his palm out to Keren. *"Postestantenum!"*

Keren closed her eyes. She hoped being blown to bits would be a quick and painless death. She sucked in another breath and wondered what was taking so long.

"Postestantenum!" Quinlin shouted again.

When nothing happened, Keren opened her eyes. Quinlin stood over her with both his palms outstretched. His face contorted into confusion, frustration, and fear.

He dropped to his knees. *"Postestantenum! Postestantenum! Postestantenum!"*

Briggs limped up behind Quinlin. He grabbed his shoulder and hoisted him to his feet. Briggs pulled his fist back, then landed a punch square on Quinlin's chin. The leader of the Dark Guild's eyes rolled to the back of his head. Briggs let him go, and Quinlin slumped to the ground.

Briggs bent down and scooped Keren into his arms.

"Jordon?" Keren asked.

"Shh," Briggs consoled her. He turned around, and she saw elf soldiers pouring onto the street. General Zaim stood next to Jordon.

"We're rounding up the sorcerers." General Zaim hesitated. "Rather, ex-sorcerers."

Relief washed over Keren. Ex-sorcerers. That meant Jewel had done it. She'd taken back the sorcerers' magic.

A roar above drew Keren's attention. Jewel's golden-scaled body snaked through the sky. An aura of multicolored lights danced around her. Her blue back hairs rippled in the wind, and her red spikes glowed with power. She circled over Keren. Even from this distance, Keren felt the Chinese dragon's stare.

"Thank you," Keren whispered.

Jewel roared again, then the lights shimmered, and she disappeared.

"Someone wants to see you," Briggs said as he turned.

A few feet away, Keren saw Sirena. Next to her stood Katrina.

"Katrina?" Keren asked. Tears streamed down her cheeks. Her sister had survived.

With a limp, Briggs walked Keren over to Katrina and Sirena. Katrina threw her arms around Briggs, trapping Keren between them. Keren felt her sister's hand press against her cheek for the first time. She nuzzled against it.

"I'm so glad you're alright," Keren said.

CHAPTER THIRTY

KEREN

K eren stared out the window at Calypso's topiary garden. A lion and an elephant stood frozen, facing one another as if in a deadly standoff. Two mermaid topiaries stood to the side, their hands reaching up to the sky. Keren imagined they were waving at Jewel. When Briggs's strong hands slipped around her waist, she leaned into him, taking in his earthy scent.

"They're waiting downstairs," he whispered into her ear. His warm breath and light kisses down her neck sent tingles through her body.

She turned to face him. "They can wait a while longer."

Her hands pressed into Briggs's taut chest. She felt his muscles shake as her hands continued up to his neck and around the back of his head. Her fingers locked into his hair. He pulled her close. When he pressed his lips to hers, breath rushed from her lungs.

A knock sounded on the door. "Hey," Ordell shouted. "What's taking so long?"

A deep chuckle vibrated in Briggs's chest. "We'll be right there," he said.

For the past two months, Briggs had stayed with Keren. During the first two weeks, he rarely left her side. She loved him more than she'd thought possible. He was her protector, her lover, and her best friend. Now they were about to start another adventure together.

He took her hand and weaved his fingers through hers. "Come on. It's time to say goodbye."

Keren resisted his pull. "I hate goodbyes. Can't we just stay here for a while longer?"

Ordell pounded on the door. "No, you can't. Get out here."

Keren puffed out a sigh. "Fine!" She shouted at the door.

After kissing Briggs on the cheek, she opened the door. She gave Ordell a pretend annoyed look. "You don't have to break down the door, you know."

"Everyone has said their goodbyes. Except for you two." Ordell smiled at her and grabbed her wrist. "Come on."

Ordell led her down the curved staircase. Briggs followed behind them. She paused when the foyer came into view. On one side stood Calypso and Gabriel. In their arms were Valentino and Hilderic, the hatchlings who had recently found the power to shift to their human forms. Valentino had his fingers wrapped in Gabriel's hair while Hilderic pulled on Calypso's nose. Pride swelled in Keren's chest. Because of her, the boys had a long and happy life ahead of them.

Next to them stood Ryota and Sirena, with their arms around one another. The unlikely pair had quickly fallen head over heels in love. Keren furrowed her brow. Maybe too quickly. Although she hoped they'd have a fairy-tale romance, she expected fireworks from the feisty duo.

Across the foyer stood her mom and Katrina. After all sorcerers had lost their magic, it took only three weeks for Shawn to arrange for her mom's release. Since then, Katrina's language skills had blossomed. Keren's mom had her arm around Katrina as she chatted with her daughter. Katrina sported a short pixy cut, and her cheeks had a healthy glow. They both looked so happy.

Keren's eyes moved to Nadria, who was squatting on the floor and rummaging through a duffle bag. Nadria had stayed by Keren's side through everything. But because of Nadria's devotion to her, Keren had almost lost her best friend. No, she quickly pushed those thoughts aside. Nadria was here, alive and well.

Keren sighed. Maybe not so well. Sadly, parts of Nadria's recuperation were unusually slow. Although her magic seemed to be intact, maybe even stronger, her body was still frail and far too thin. With Ordell's constant care, Keren hoped Nadria would enjoy a full recovery. A warm feeling passed through Keren's chest as she fought back tears. No, this was a happy occasion. The time for tears was over.

"Come on." Ordell pulled on her wrist.

They finished walking the rest of the way downstairs.

"Keren," Calypso said.

When Keren walked up to Calypso, Hilderic smashed his hand into his father's face. Unable to stop herself, Keren let out an amused giggle. She covered her mouth and hoped Calypso hadn't taken offense.

The dragon warlord gave his son's hand a soft kiss, then set him on the ground. Valentino wiggled in Gabriel's arms until she set him down next to his brother.

"Well," Calypso said as he rubbed the red handprint on his cheek, "he has my spunk."

Gabriel smiled and radiated delight as she watched the twins play together. "They both do." She gave Calypso a kiss on his injured cheek.

Calypso shook his head and sighed as he watched his sons play. "We have our hands full, Gabriel." Then his adoring eyes met his mate's. "Well, at least they've inherited their mother's beauty." He brushed his hand along Gabriel's jawline.

Gabriel held Calypso's gaze for a long moment. Keren could feel the intense love radiating from the couple. With Briggs, she was just beginning to understand this type of deep love and adoration.

Then Gabriel stepped up to Keren. "Thank you for saving my family." She gave Keren a kiss on the cheek.

Gabriel's soft lips sent a wave of warmth through Keren's body. Pushing between their legs, Valentino and Hilderic rushed outside.

"Boys!" Gabriel shouted. "Stay close to the house." She chuckled, shook her head, and gave Keren a warm smile before trotting after the twins.

Calypso's voice took on a stern tone. "The world is changing. I feel magic transforming itself."

Keren startled at the change in mood. "Transforming itself? I'm not sure I understand." Keren felt lost and exposed when the others talked about magic. She'd been part of their circle. Now she was just a normal human.

"The push and pull of magic these past months has caused a palpable shift. I don't understand exactly what's happening." Calypso put a hand on Keren's arm. "We must keep in contact."

Keren's stomach rolled. Everything she'd done over the last several months continued to reshape magic. Without magic of her own, she had no insight into what was happening.

She looked at Briggs. His somber look worried her. She reached a hand out to him. When he entwined his fingers with hers, the warmth comforted her rising fear and doubt. With Briggs, her family, and her friends on her side, they'd survive anything.

"I feel it too," Briggs said. With a nod, he added, "We'll check in. If anything happens here, contact us."

"I will." Calypso gave Briggs a half smile and held out his hand. "Briggs Wilson," he tipped his head to the side. "Our relationship has been," he thought for a moment, "turbulent. However, I've grown to respect you, and I hope we can put the past behind us."

Briggs slapped his hand into Calypso's. "Consider it behind us." He glanced at Keren. "Thank you for everything you've done for Keren."

"It has been an honor and a pleasure," the dragon warlord said as he gave Keren a slight bow.

Keren felt her cheeks flush. Compliments made her feel self-conscious and a little embarrassed. Luckily, Jerold saved her from the uncomfortable situation when he stepped into the foyer and banged on the open door. He was Gaines's right-hand man in the PIB.

"Come on, people. We don't have all day." The wide, cheery grin on Jerold's face helped Keren relax. Everyone walked outside.

Several feet from the house were three PIB agents in their dragon form. Gaines gave a flourished bow, then said, "Your carriages await."

"Gaines," Keren said. She ran up to him and put her arms around the puca, giving him a tight squeeze. "How can I thank you?"

Gaines grinned. "We're a team. Thanks aren't necessary."

"We have one more bag," Ordell said as he handed Nadria's duffle to Jerold.

Jerold took the bag. "Don't be a stranger, Ordell." He rubbed his chin and frowned in a teasing way. "Are you sure you don't want to join the PIB?"

Ordell smiled. "No, but it's a tempting offer. Maybe after I graduate."

"Or maybe not," Nadria whispered as she stepped next to Keren.

Keren laughed, then turned to face Nadria's large, pale-blue eyes. Her heart clenched seeing the premature wrinkles at the edges. "I'll miss you."

Nadria smiled. "I'll miss you too. But it won't be too long." She held up her left hand with her fingers splayed. A single diamond shimmered on a slim gold band on Nadria's ring finger. "You're my maid of honor."

Tears welled in Keren's eyes. "I'm so happy for you."

Nadria giggled. "Thanks." She turned her hand so she could see the ring. "We have everything planned. We'll live with Mama Murphy while Ordell finishes college. I'll pick up my magic studies as soon as we fix the damage in the Magic Underground. I'm planning fundraisers to help with the effort."

Keren shook her head and smiled. "Of course you are."

Nadria laughed. It was a light-hearted laugh Keren hadn't heard from her best friend for quite some time.

"Next year," Keren said. "Briggs and I will be in Orlando for Ordell's graduation and your wedding."

Nadria squealed. "My wedding." She flung her arms around Keren's neck.

Over Nadria's shoulder, Keren saw Briggs with Ordell. He gave Ordell a pat on the back and a handshake. Ordell's grin showed he was pleased. Briggs looked away, trying to hide his tears.

"Come on," Ordell called out to Nadria. "Mama's waiting. She's excited to see us."

Keren kissed Nadria's cheek and fought back tears as she waved goodbye.

Nadria and Ordell climbed onto an agent's back. The other agent had their bags. As both pucas took to the sky, Keren wished she were going to Orlando with her friends. She pictured the four of them curled up on a couch, snuggled under a blanket. They'd be sharing a bowl of popcorn and laughing at the way a B horror movie failed at jump scares. She watched until the dragons disappeared into the distance.

"Keren?" Sirena's soft voice startled her back to the moment.

She turned to see the Elf Princess's beaming face. Instead of medieval attire, Sirena wore jeans and a light-blue tank top. Both showed off her soft curves. The teenager had grown into a woman.

"We're going now." Sirena took Keren's hand. "I'll miss you." Then she frowned. "Promise to visit."

Keren laughed. "I promise."

"No." Sirena flicked Keren's elf ear, then said in her stern I'm-the-Elf Princess voice. "Promise. Sister promise." Then Sirena let out a mirthful laugh.

"I sister promise." Keren sighed as she put a hand on Sirena's cheek. Maybe she wasn't quite a woman yet. "Take care of yourself."

Sirena's face glowed with happiness. "Once we're settled, I'll contact you."

"Sounds good." Keren gave Sirena a hug and watched her walk back to Ryota.

"You take care of her," Keren shouted to Ryota. "Or you'll have me to deal with."

Ryota raised his eyebrows as he tapped his herringbone newsboy hat. He gave Keren a slight nod. Then he stepped back and shifted into an elegant orange dragon. He puffed out a cloud of smoke, then pushed his nose into Sirena's hand. The Elf Princess caressed him, then gave him a kiss. She climbed up on his back and waved to everyone. With a roar, Ryota took to the air. The wind from his strong wings blew Keren's hair back as she watched them leave.

"They make an interesting pair," Calypso said.

"Yes, they do." Keren rubbed the back of her neck. "Do you think it was a good idea to let them go?" She turned to Calypso. "I mean, shouldn't all the dragons have stayed here with you?"

Calypso took a deep breath before answering. "Ryota has always dreamed of living a more secluded life. He is fiercely loyal to me and would never have left without permission."

"But the other dragons?" Keren asked.

With a shrug, Calypso sighed. "A few wanted the same thing. Who am I to keep them here against their will? Besides, they'll all be back during mating season."

Keren wanted to know how Calypso felt about the new power couple. "Do you approve of Ryota and Sirena?"

"Ryota's mate died soon after the sorcerers imprisoned us. Now, with no other available dragon females, mating out of his race seems logical. Also, the elves want the same secluded life." He crossed his arms. "Besides, with this agreement, we've moved the elves to an isolated area of the world, and Las Vegas can return to normal."

Under Calypso's watchful eye, Keren knew Las Vegas would heal and return to its former glory.

Keren eyed Calypso. "So, their relationship is a strategic move for you?"

He gave her a half smile. "Shouldn't everything be strategic, Keren Stewart?"

Before she could answer, Valentino and Hilderic rushed over.

"My boys," Calypso said as he scooped them into his arms. "Say goodbye to Auntie Keren."

"Auntie Keren?" She smiled. "Is that strategic?"

With a shrug, Calypso laughed. "You figure it out."

Both hatchlings gave Keren a kiss. Then Calypso turned to her. "You are like family to me and Gabriel. You're always welcome."

"Thanks. That means a lot." She kissed each of the hatchlings. "I love you. Be good." Then she pointed a finger at them. "Give your dad a hard time."

"Auntie's only kidding," Calypso said as he put the hatchlings down. He patted them lightly on their backs. "Go find Mommy." The boys scampered away.

Gaines and Briggs walked over. "Are you ready?" Gaines asked.

"I am." Keren looked around. "Where's Jerold?"

"He went back to the office," Gaines said. "He hates long goodbyes."

It surprised Keren that she, Briggs, Katrina, and her mom would fly on two puca dragons. Especially all the way to New Jersey. "We're all riding double?"

"Look up," Calypso said as he pointed to the sky.

Keren looked to where he pointed. Soon, another dragon came into view. As it flew closer, Keren saw it was only slightly smaller than Calypso's dragon form. It must be a male since females weren't that large. She didn't recognize him. The dragon circled overhead, then made a soft landing on the driveway. Shimmering silver scales covered his body and his thickset chest puffed out.

"Your escort," Calypso said. "But don't keep him long in New Jersey. Petrov is replacing Ryota as my chauffer."

"*Petrov*?" Keren exclaimed. "But I thought ... you know."

"When you brought all dragon magic back to this realm, Petrov found his flame. He's been practicing his shift and wanted to surprise you." Calypso motioned to Petrov. "Go see him."

With a grunt, Petrov turned to face Keren. She walked over, and he lowered his head to look into her eyes. Reaching out, she put her hand on his warm nose. "I'm so happy for you, Petrov."

The giant, intimidating beast purred into her hand.

"Go on," Calypso said with an exasperated tone. "This is taking far too long."

Keren turned, and in three strides had her arms wrapped around Calypso's neck. "Thank you for everything."

"Yes," he said as he tugged her arms off him. Calypso's face was bright red as he stepped back. He straightened his shirt and cleared his throat. "Tell me. Why did you choose New Jersey?"

Well, well, the great dragon warlord can be embarrassed, Keren thought. It was sort of sweet. "Mom got a job offer from Princeton University. They're the number one school for linguistics studies."

"And what about your boyfriend?"

"The college offered Briggs a position in the Social Sciences department."

Calypso raised an eyebrow. "I can't picture Briggs as a teacher."

"Please don't. That would be a total disaster," Briggs said as he put his arm around Keren. "I'm overseeing the curriculum for police and compliance officers."

Calypso nodded, then stepped back, probably trying to avoid another impromptu hug. "Well, good luck. I wish you both the best." He pointed to the puca dragons. "Your mom and sister are ready to go."

Keren turned to see Katrina perched on the PIB agent's back. Gaines had transformed into his dragon form. Her mom, looking tentative, clung to his back.

Briggs climbed onto Petrov's back and offered Keren a hand up. Once they settled, Keren looked back and gave Calypso and Gabriel a final wave.

"Let's go," Keren said.

Petrov took to the sky. He circled over Calypso's mansion, then followed the puca dragons east. Keren closed her eyes, letting the cool breeze blow across her face.

If you enjoyed *Magic Transformed: Twisted Curse Book Four*, please consider leaving a review at http://www.amazon.com/review/create-review?&asin=B0B7GMV4SV or use the QR code below. Reviews make a difference and I'm grateful for your support. Simply a line or two is all you need.

Go to **Amazon** and grab your copies of the complete *Twisted Curse* series today!

V isit **https://www.djdalton.com**, or use the QR code below, and subscribe to my newsletter to receive updates on new releases as well as other freebies. As a subscriber, you'll receive access to the free download of the novella prequel to the *Twisted Curse Series*, *The Dragon War*.

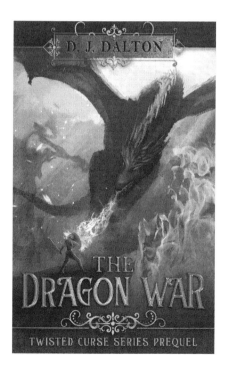

About the Author

On a crisp Michigan day after a snowstorm, I watched a snowplow bury my car just moments after shoveling a way clear to leave for work. By the end of that year, I had arranged a work transfer to our Florida office. Leaving my winter coat and mittens behind, I settled in central Florida where I live today with my family.

I enjoy being active and am always looking for the next glorious adventure. From Tae Kwon Do to dancing, or tumbling around in an adult gymnastics class, I look for physical and mental challenges to grow and enrich my life.

Visit me at my website https://www.djdalton.com or use the QR code above.

f facebook.com/profile.php?id=100067778113765

a amazon.com/~/e/B09B5PRLHD

g goodreads.com/author/show/21681309.D_J_Dalton

BB bookbub.com/authors/d-j-dalton

Made in the USA
Columbia, SC
05 September 2022

66651679R00114